With Gladness:
A Christmas Story Collection

Peace + Joy !

Sarah Kay Bierle

Sarah Kay Bierle

Gazette665

To Madeleine

Wishing you a joyous and beautiful Christmas,
this year and always.

CONTENTS

INTRODUCTION

As with gladness men of old
Did the guiding star behold;
As with joy they hailed its light,
Leading onward, beaming bright,
So, most gracious Lord, may we
Evermore be led to Thee.
~ William C. Dix

It's hard to choose a favorite season, but Christmas holds a special place in many hearts. I have fond memories of decorating the house, baking cookies for neighbors, and making gifts, but my favorite "childhood" Christmas memories are reading aloud with my family and creating grand dramatic productions.

Sitting cozily on the couch near the Christmas tree, my dad would read from the Bible or a holiday story. Our collection of advent books grew through the years and now takes several storage boxes! As I grew older and started my studies as a historian, I began looking for accounts about holiday celebrations in different eras and found many special moments as people around the world celebrated the birth of the Savior.

However, I wasn't content to just read about Christmases of long ago. I wanted to "recreate" them – find a way to share the inspiration. My brothers will forever accuse me of having a flair for drama. I would write scripts; they would design sets and special effects. Together, we'd learn our lines, squabble, design tickets and programs, and eventually put on a presentation in our living room for our parents. Special times and memories that I'll always treasure, especially now that we're grown and won't always be together for holidays.

This collection of Christmas stories was a joy to create. *Patriot's Dream* is very loosely based on one of the plays we performed. Other stories came from outline drafts of performances I wanted to write, but didn't have the opportunity (or sibling support) for the idea. Others are newly crafted plots in "rediscovered" days of the past.

While the settings of the stories are historical and as accurate as possible, the main characters and story details are completely fictional. There are historical notes at the back of this book, giving further explanation and sharing some of my original inspiration.

It's my hope – whether you read this book aloud with your family, with a friend, or quietly on your own – you'll be blessed and inspired. Always gather favorite memories from the best moments in life – some of my most treasured feelings and thoughts are woven into these stories.

Over 2,000 years ago, shepherds and wise men went "with gladness" to find the newborn Savior in a manger bed. In the last couple hundred years, other "men of old" celebrated Christmas - upholding traditions, searching for peace, finding forgiveness, and clinging to hope. These stories pay respectful tribute to those moments and celebrations in America's past...and will hopefully inspire you in the "leading onward" years to meet each day with simple gladness.

GREAT JOY

1700'S

COLONIAL ERA

GREAT JOY

This was not his idea of a pleasant Christmas Eve. The snow drifted and swirled, forcing Michael Robertson to pull his cloak tighter and push his crushed hat lower over his face. Chased out of the festively decorated town on a winter's night was not his idea of a jolly good time. He tried to be thankful for the small blessing: he was out of prison. The air was clean, even if it was cold. Step after step in the powdery snow with no idea what to do.

Three months ago, life had been filled with happy routine. Michael had been a journeyman tailor in the capital city, perfecting his skills crafting fine suits for the wealthy men in the community. Then rumors swirled with the autumn leaves. A false accusation of stealing a large sum of money. His arrest and soul-searching days in prison. The day on trial before the jury in the courthouse. The smirk on the oafish apprentice's face as the sentence was read: hanging at the next execution day.

That self-satisfied smirk had untangled the

confusion in his innocent mind. The apprentice had been disgruntled when Michael was hired as a journeyman in the shop – a position the older apprentice had expected to receive, despite his notoriously poor workmanship. The theft had been rigged to point to Michael, but he had no way to prove it and no witnesses on his side.

Frustrated desperation had plagued him during the long days and nights in the stinking cell. How could he prove his innocence? As a fairly recent arrival in the capital city, he did not have life-long friends to testify of his good character. Alone, he waited for the day when the sentence would be carried out.

Then this afternoon, the jailer entered the cell, announcing Michael Robertson was innocent and free. A magistrate had explained that while most of the witnesses had told the truth about what they saw, one had lied. The liar had confessed on his sick bed, hours before his death.

Michael was free. As he strode from prison, he had noticed the charming holiday decorations – evergreen, pinecone, moss, and vine wreaths and swags, accented with fruits, seed pods, other natural items, and yards of ribbon looped into puffy bows. The shops had filled their front windows with lovely gift ideas while the town house doorways were festooned with garlands. However, the citizens' hearts had not been as cheery as the exterior of their town. Rowdy boys and tavern drunks – unwilling to believe the truth – had chased Michael down the wide main street, pelting snowballs and stones at him while the quality folk watched with smirks and giggles.

There would be no warm welcome or

comfortable chair by an inn fire in the capital city tonight, so he trudged into the countryside. His feelings were muddled: relief, thankfulness, resentment, concern for the future. He didn't have family, didn't have anyone to visit, no faithful friend. It was a disadvantage, being a new arrival in the colony last year. The twilight deepened into darkness, and his soaked shoes and stockings made icy pain with every step.

"I'll have to find some shelter. A barn or something," he mumbled to himself. "Too cold to go on." A short wall appeared along the left side of the road, then the entrance to an avenue. Michael saw the brightly lit windows of a small home. "A farmhouse, I suppose. They wouldn't want me there, but they just might have a good stable." Wearily, he moved up the lane, skirted the house with its evergreen bedecked door, and spotted the barn.

"Who are you?" called a little voice. Michael jumped and glanced around quickly. "I'm here!" the voice shouted again. Looking up, he saw a boy peering curiously through a half-raised window. Before he could think of a reply, the boy went on. "Can you come in? Papa's going to read the Christmas story."

"Uh, no. I wasn't invited."

"I'll ask Mama if you can come in!" The window slammed shut. Michael ran, not sure what to do.

"Halloo," a man shouted from the back door. "Who's there?"

Michael stopped. He didn't have anything to run from, he scolded himself. But weeks in the jail – despite his innocence – had made him feel like a criminal, unwanted and unwelcomed.

"A traveler, sir." Michael turned and went toward the back door where a tall man stood waiting. "I'm Michael Robertson," he said, extending his hand to shake the stranger's.

"Mr. Robertson. What brings you out on such a cold Christmas Eve?"

"I'm traveling." In the light from the back window, Michael noticed the gentleman's friendly smile and plain, finely tailored coat. I made that green coat, he thought miserably, realizing how much the accusations and prior months had taken from him. Work, opportunity, social position, honor.

"You wouldn't happen to be Michael Robertson, the journeyman in the tailor's shop?" the man asked, scrutinizing him carefully. "I'm George Fuller. Not sure if you'll remember me. I was in the shop last spring."

"Yes, sir."

"And I suppose you'll tell me that you're on a midnight stroll before you return to your cell?" Michael stiffened. "No, don't look like that, Mr. Robertson. My father-in-law was in town today and brought back the report of what had happened. Forgive me, it was a bad jest."

"Papa, are you coming in?" a girl's high voice called through the closed door.

"Come join us," Mr. Fuller said, putting his hand on Michael's shoulder.

"I'm hardly dressed for company," he excused. "If I could just sleep in the stable, that would be fine."

"Nonsense. It's just my little family, and we've not even done much decorating – just what the children and I could manage. The relatives couldn't come this year, and my wife is getting over a sickness, so we couldn't travel either. I'm cold, and you must be too. Come on." Reluctantly, Michael allowed himself to be led inside.

In the main room, a warm fire crackled on the hearth. Evergreen boughs accented with rosy apples decorated the mantle. On the chimney, a wreath twined of dried vines featured a decorative display of dried orange slices and spices, filling the room with a homey scent.

"Come, sit by the fire," invited a thin woman from her blanket-lined chair. "You must be chilled through. I'm sorry for not rising to greet you properly."

"Don't trouble yourself, ma'am," Michael said. "I appreciate your hospitality. Especially taking in a stranger." She smiled and motioned him to take a chair near the blazing warmth.

The four children lined up and stared at him curiously until their father instructed them to "mind your manners." The oldest girl – Meg – introduced her siblings Nathaniel, Archie, and Jane, and then offered to get Michael some hot tea.

Enjoying the warm drink, Michael started to relax. Young Archie sat on the wood floor near him, watching. "It's too bad he's not a robber," he whispered loudly.

"Archie, that's unkind," Mrs. Fuller said, while Mr. Fuller shook his head and cleared his throat.

"I didn't mean anything bad, Papa. It's just if he was a robber, it would've been more exciting, and you would've had to fire your gun to keep us all safe."

Michael covered his face with his hand. How

was he ever going to rebuild his reputation and find work if even a six year old child believed he was guilty? It would have been better to stay in the snow. Maybe drift into the sleep of the dead.

"Hush, Archie," Meg ordered, echoed by stern words from Mr. Fuller.

"He doesn't know what he was saying," Mr. Fuller said. "Please don't leave."

"I think I must." Michael stood up, heading for the door and the cold night. "I'll only ruin your Christmas Eve."

Before the host or hostess could say anything, Archie ran to Michael. "Don't go. I'm sorry if I said something bad. It's just that Father's been showing Nate and I how to load the gun in case an animal or bad man comes. But now I know you're not a bad man, 'cause Papa wouldn't have let you in the house, if you were. You must be a very good man. Please stay. I'm sorry." Archie grabbed his hand and wouldn't let go.

You must be a very good man...the phrase etched in Michael's mind. "I'll stay," he promised the anxious little boy, then knelt down to the child's height. "But everyone thinks I'm a bad man. They think I'm a robber."

"But you're not!" Archie protested. "Papa wouldn't be friends with a robber. Would you?" he asked turning toward his parents.

"Come here, son," Mr. Fuller said, "and listen, all of you children. It is easy to make assumptions and believe rumors about people. But we have to learn the truth before we make judgments. Mr. Robertson needs some friends. He needs people to stand by him and help him. Are we willing to do that?" The children nodded. "Mr. Robertson, will you stay with us at least for the next couple days?"

"We'll make you happy," Archie promised.

"I'll stay. I can do some work for you." Michael glanced down. "But I don't know if I'll be joyful company for the holidays."

"Just join us," Mr. Fuller said. "And now – if I can find my spectacles – we were going to read the Christmas story from the Bible." With the children gathered around, he read the account from the Gospel of Luke. Each of the children commented on their favorite part of the story, and their parents added words of wisdom.

When it was his turn, Archie announced, "My favorite part is where the angel says not to be afraid because there is such joyful news. Baby Jesus had come, and everyone was happy."

"Those are wonderful words of hope," Mrs. Fuller replied.

"What did Jesus do when He grew up?" Mr. Fuller quizzed his children.

"Healed people," Meg answered quickly, squeezing her mother's hand.

"Played with children," Jane lisped.

"Well, we know He blessed them," her father corrected.

"Died on the cross," Nathaniel said.

Archie thought for a while. "Had dinner with people that other people didn't like."

"What do you mean?" Mrs. Fuller asked.

"Remember, Papa was reading it. About when Jesus had dinner with the tax men and bad people, and the religious men didn't like it. But were they really bad people, Papa? It seems like Jesus wouldn't want people to be bad."

Michael shifted nervously in his seat, not entirely comfortable with the conversation and nervous about Mr. Fuller's response.

"No, son, Jesus doesn't want people to do bad things. But He did take the time to talk with those tax collectors that no one else wanted to help. He was able to tell them the truth and point them to repentance and God. Sometimes, there are people who others don't want to associate with. But, sometimes, those are the very people who need a kind word and helping hand."

"So they will be happy?" Archie finished, and his father nodded.

Mr. Fuller had not glanced at Michael as he spoke and had not implied that Michael was wicked or needed special help. Instead, the words comforted him. Michael was able to sing some of the merry songs and then said good-night to the children as they prepared to go upstairs.

"Tomorrow," Mr. Fuller said, "we're going to hitch up the horses and go to church in town, as long as the snow doesn't get deeper. Would you like to go with us?"

"Oh, I don't think so," Michael responded, rubbing at a worn patch on his coat cuff.

"My wife's father is an influential landowner. We will be sitting in the family pew at church. And you would sit with us."

"Your father-in-law would not want me there, if he knew."

"You're wrong about that. He told me he wished he could help you after seeing what happened when you were released."

"Why would your family do this? Help me?" Michael asked. "Don't you care what people will think?"

"Did Christ care what the hypocritical Pharisees thought when He took the good news to the tax collectors? Come with us. People must eventually learn the truth about the false accusation. If you are innocent, why run away?"

I can't do this, Michael thought the next morning as he sat in the wagon. The Fuller Family and Mr. and Mrs. Ward were conversing by the church door. He had asked for just a moment alone. His hands were sweating, and he wanted to run. Already, a few townspeople had stared at him suspiciously.

"Are you coming?" Archie called, climbing up on the wagon wheel. "We're going to sing in church. And last night you said you liked to sing."

"I guess I'll come." Michael jumped down, straightened his coat, bowed his head, and started walking toward the door.

He felt a little hand slip into his, and Archie smiled up at him. "Remember, you're a very good man. And you're my friend," the lad whispered.

Michael's eyes got misty. He blinked quickly, then stood tall, and lifted his head.

The half-dozen townsfolk gathered near the door stared. "Mr. Ward," called one impertinent gossip, "just look who's coming with your grandson."

The tall, older gentleman turned. "Ah, yes. Come join us, Mr. Robertson. Glad to see you today." Mr. Ward stepped into the foyer of the church.

"Did you know he's a robber?" the same noisy gossip hissed to Archie.

Michael wanted to retreat, to avoid embarrassing the little boy or the kind family. He started to turn away, but Archie held his hand tightly.

"Mr. Robertson's a good man," Archie said, his voice a little shrill as he tried to speak loudly. "And whether he's a robber or not, he needs our help. My Papa says that's why Jesus came to earth – to help others. Can't you do that today? Especially since it's Christmas?"

Michael saw the townspeople's wide eyes, open mouths, and accusing fingers, but Archie pulled him into the church foyer before anyone else could respond. "Um, I don't think I should go in the sanctuary," Michael said, trying desperately to get away before the next person came with gossipy insults.

"It's alright," Archie said, trying to push open the heavy inner doors. "Just remember what the angels said, *'Don't be afraid, for behold, I bring you good tidings of great joy... For there is born to you this day in the city of David a Savior, who is Christ the Lord.'*"

Michael took a deep breath and pushed open the sanctuary door. "Don't be afraid," he told himself.

The congregation stared. They pointed. They whispered. Michael kept his head up and sat down beside the Fullers and the Wards.

"I heard it was all a mistake," whispered one lady loudly in the next pew. "He was really innocent. I heard it from the judge himself." The news buzzed and swirled before the service began. Michael tried to ignore it, focusing on the Christmas greenery draped around the tall windows and pulpit. Intently, he studied the sprigs of holly tied with red ribbon and hung on the pews.

Just as the minister stood up, one couple came in, bustling to take their seats in the pew behind Michael. He hadn't paid much attention to them until the man tapped him on the arm. It was the tailor, his former employer. "Michael, I'm real sorry about all that happened. In God's house, I can't say what I'd like to do to that apprentice. I was afraid you'd left town. Spent all last night looking for you. If you can forgive me, will you come back and work in my shop?"

"Thank you," Michael managed to say. He couldn't believe that his employer had actually gone looking for him. Perhaps the world was not as dark and gloomy as he thought. Perhaps real friends made all the difference. "I think I can try to forget what happened. I'd be happy to come back to work."

"Good. Good. That's a right Christian attitude. And I thank you."

The minister came to the front of the church and announced the first song. As they stood, Archie tugged on Michael's coat and said triumphantly. "See, I told you. Don't be afraid."

"Yes," Michael replied, feeling the warmth of forgiveness and trust. He inhaled the rich scent of pine boughs in the chilly air and glanced at his new friends. Smiling, he whispered to himself, "And there's great joy."

Sarah Kay Bierle

PATRIOT DREAMS

WINTER 1778

AMERICAN WAR FOR INDEPENDENCE

Sarah Kay Bierle

PATRIOT DREAMS

"Nearly there," Hannah murmured, adjusting the reins in her cold hands and guiding the tired horse as the wagon rolled through the icy snow. For the second year in a row, she was arriving at the winter camp of the Continental Army. On either side of the road, men crouched around fires or hurried into the frail log huts they had constructed.

Hannah had almost decided not to come this winter. It was difficult to travel, and she worried about the farm when she was away. The letter that had prompted this visit was hidden deep in her pocket, beneath the layers of clothes and capes. Major Patton – her husband – had written with such disappointment and despair she knew she had to go. In the safety of home, she had wondered how he could've lost faith in the cause of independence. Here, seeing the bloody footprints in the snow, the weariness and hunger, and the gloomily defeated spirits, she began to understand his attitude.

"Mrs. Patton?" inquired a low, recognizable voice. Glancing behind her as she halted the horse, she saw her husband, holding his tricorn hat in his hands while the wind tousled his dark hair.

"Ezekiel," she whispered, smiling. She took his hand and stepped down from the wagon. Hannah noticed they were closely watched by the soldiers who paced in the snow or loitered in forlorn groups.

"You are here much sooner than I expected. Come into the cabin. Out of the cold." Tucking her gloved hand in his arm with a look of proud possession, Ezekiel led her toward a tiny hut with a smoky chimney.

The cabin's interior was sparse, but it was shelter. By the dim light of a fire on the hearth, she saw the silhouetted figures of other officers. "Mrs. Patton has arrived gentlemen. My lieutenants, Hannah. We were preparing for a meeting. Supplies are low and..." he paused, as though wondering if she cared about their troubles.

"Good day." She nodded to the officers, then continued. "I've brought some food and clothing in the wagon. The ladies at the village and I have been busy. Perhaps it will help?"

She couldn't see their expressions in the dark room, but she felt their relief when they heard her words. "Thank you, ma'am." The speaker stood up. "Perhaps we could unload the wagon for you." They headed for the door.

"You are more efficient than Congress, my dear," Ezekiel murmured.

"What do you mean?" Hannah laughed, as the last lieutenant stepped out and closed the door.

"Never mind that." He pushed back her hood

and leaned down to kiss her. "I'm glad you are here. So thankful."

Late that night, after dining with the four lieutenants and three sergeants who managed to squeeze into the cabin, Hannah sat near the fire, watching her silent husband. Ezekiel declined talking about the military challenges and had only asked briefly about their farm. The flames in the fireplace subdued to glowing coals. Hannah shivered, realizing the light of patriotism was burning dangerously low; it seemed like a sudden flurry of snow might extinguish it forever.

"You will call on Lady Washington?" Ezekiel asked the next morning, stepping into the chilly air and helping Hannah fasten the troublesome clasp on her brown cape.

As they walked through the snow toward the stone building which served as official headquarters and General and Lady Washington's residence, Hannah glanced at her husband. He was lost in his own world of troubles. Was he regretting the decisions they had made to support the patriot cause? The promises and discussions they had shared in past years?

Pushing aside those thoughts, Hannah forced a charming smile as they entered the headquarters building. In the sitting room, Lady Washington and Mrs. Greene greeted her pleasantly, and Ezekiel left her after a polite bow and the proper words to the other ladies. They settled with their knitting and discussed the news of the previous year.

"Is Major Patton well?" Mrs. Greene asked after a while. "We have been concerned, but didn't think we should pester him with too many inquiries."

Sighing, Hannah laid down her knitting needles and pressed her hands together. "I don't know. Something is different. He does not want to talk. Last winter when I came to camp, we talked about everything. I copied messages and reports for him, and I was happy to do it. But now...it's like he's hiding something."

"There are times in the last weeks when I've thought the same about my husband," Mrs. Greene admitted.

After a pause, Lady Washington said quietly, "If I may observe, ladies... It was a hard year for everyone, and these early months of 1778 have not brought improvements. Defeat takes its toll, even on great commanders. And now the army is forced into lonely winter quarters." She looked at Hannah. "If you are brave enough, walk through the camp. You will see." Then she turned the conversation to a pleasant topic.

In the afternoon, Hannah ventured out of the dark cabin, intending to take some provisions to her husband's unit. Not far from the doorway, a soldier huddled on a tree stump, tying his worn scarf over his battered hat. "Good afternoon," she said pleasantly. "Would you like some cornbread and something warm to drink?"

"Huh?" the soldier responded. "Oh, good day. Yes. Please." He fumbled in his carry-all bag and pulled out a tin cup.

"It's just some hot apple cider. Nothing fancy, but it's warm. And here," Hannah lifted the cover on the basket, "have something to eat."

Suspicion clouded the soldier's blue eyes, and he hesitated, rubbing his dark beard. "Are you a spy, lady?"

"Goodness, no! I'm only trying to help."

"That's kind of you. But there's hundreds of us, and we're all starving."

"I know, but I'm here to assist. If each person would help and support our cause in the best way they can, then I have every confidence this war will end soon."

The soldier stared at her in disbelief. "You really think that ma'am? Still?" Hannah nodded. "If you don't mind my asking ma'am, what would you do if you saw your best friend get killed at the Brandywine battle, and you just don't believe anymore?"

Hannah glanced away for a second, praying for the right words. "I think," she began sympathetically.

"Well, lady, you can think all you like, but I know what I'm goin' to do." He stood up, towering over Hannah. "There ain't no hope for this cause and army. Starvin', freezin', and Lord Howe's got our capital." He scuffed at the snow with his cracking boots. "Sorry, but this ain't liberty. I'm done fightin'. There ain't any heroes, and Private Isaac Hammond is goin' home!" He turned and started marching away.

"Wait..." Hannah called, following him. "Listen to me. Heroes don't fall from heaven or appear from thin air. They are the men who are determined and who persevere with courage." Though she feared it was a useless appeal, Hannah went on. "What will the world say, what will the generations that come after us say, what will history say about us? Will they look at our struggle and say, 'See, self-government fails. Our forefathers gave up because it was hard. Or...it was a struggle with good intentions for liberty, but it failed because they got disheartened and quit.' What will they say about us? Are we cowards or heroes?"

Private Hammond shrugged. "Heroes always win. Like I said, we haven't..."

"No," Hannah insisted. "Heroes don't always win, but, when they lose, they try again. Only cowards flee." Her expression dared him to contradict.

"Someone else can stay and be a hero. I'm goin' home."

"Alright. Each person makes a choice. It looks like you've made yours. Just remember, every cause needs men who will never give up, even when the struggle is hard." Hannah turned and started walking away.

"Excuse me," the soldier called. Hannah stopped. "If you're so charitable, you might want to look in that first hut. A comrade's real sick. And who are you?"

Hannah looked back. "Thank you. I'll go. I'm Mrs. Patton, Major Patton's wife."

Private Hammond chuckled wickedly. "If you want to preach about heroism, get your husband to listen. I expect him to be leaving any day too."

Hannah gasped and covered her mouth with her hand. Then it was true. Her impression and fears were not without foundation. If a common soldier had recognized the hesitation and despair in her husband... "I have to talk to him. No," she corrected herself, "he has to talk to me." Squaring her shoulders, she walked toward the shaky lean-to.

"Good day," she called softly, pushing open the door. "Is anyone here?"

From the dark interior, she heard a cough, then a weak voice. "Here, in the corner."

"I've brought food. Would you like some?"

"Yes, yes please. There's kindling by the door, if you want light."

Hannah coaxed the glowing embers to life, and soon the fire cast a flickering light in the tiny shelter. She handed some cornbread to the pale young soldier, asking, "Can I do anything else for you?"

"Sit and talk, if you have the time and courage."

"You don't look very frightening, and I can't image you have too many dark secrets," Hannah said playfully, making him smile. She waited a moment, noticing his pallor and feverish look. "How long have you been ill?"

"Like this for a week, but not well for a month."

"I brought some medicines. I could bring them here for you," she offered, and he nodded. "How long have you served in the army?"

"Since the beginning. Two and a half years. I'm sorry I won't live to see the end."

Hannah shook her head. "Now, don't talk like that. You may recover yet."

He smiled again. "You are kind."

"Do you have family? Would you like me to write a letter for you?"

The soldier brushed the cornbread crumbs off his blanket. "Thank you, no. I wrote a few days ago." He studied her in the dim light. "You look familiar, ma'am. Have we met before?"

"Perhaps." Hannah brushed a loose strand of her long hair back under her linen cap. "I'm Mrs.

Patton – the Major's wife. Your name?"

"Matthew Neal, corporal in the Continental Army, and right proud of the fact. Fought at Princeton last year and other battles too. It was an honor to serve in Major Patton's unit this summer and autumn. He is a fine soldier and real patriot."

Hannah felt unsure; she knew Corporal Neal's words were true a year ago, but she had a grim foreboding that Major Patton was not devoted to their cause any longer. But this was not something she would discuss with a stranger. "You're a good soldier, Corporal Neal."

"Tried my best, ma'am." Corporal Neal shrugged. "Looking at my life, I'm rather satisfied. Nothing to be ashamed of. No regrets. There's only one thing I wonder..." He paused and seemed unwilling to go on.

"And what is that, corporal?" Hannah asked gently.

He sighed. "I'm no philosopher, but I can't help wondering. Three hundred years from now, what will they say about us? Will they call us radical rebels? Old-fashioned men with morals and faith that they will think is outdated? What will be the legacy of all these sacrifices? What will history say about us? Do you know what I mean, ma'am?"

"Yes, I understand," Hannah replied, pressing her hands together and steadying her voice. "I only pray they will tell the truth."

"Indeed." Corporal Neal leaned back, looking toward the dark roof and seeming to forget she was there. "And what will that truth be? That our cause ended at a place called Valley Forge because courage and hope died. Or that we came through and went on and on until our flag flies in every part of this land...and we are truly free. And then what? What will our nation be?" He exhaled gently and closed his eyes, then breathed again shallowly.

Hannah wanted to give him hope, answering quietly, "Our nation will be whatever our people are. It is the citizens that make a nation. Surely the blessing of Providence will be on a nation whose people put their trust in Him. Surely He will make that nation prosper."

"I believe you are right," Corporal Neal said, looking at her again. "Your words seem almost like an angel's prophesy..."

"Oh no!" Hannah exclaimed, embarrassed. "It is only my hope and prayer."

"It is a wonderful hope for the future." His eyes started to close again, but he struggled to stay awake, finally saying, "I'm sorry, but I'm exhausted. I..."

"I'll leave you to rest. May God bless you, Corporal Neal."

"You've encouraged me, and I will include you in my prayers."

"I would be honored to have your prayers. But please pray mostly for our country and its leaders. Especially Major Patton," Hannah added in an undertone. "Rest well. Our army and country need more men of faith and courage."

In the late evening, Ezekiel and Hannah walked from headquarters through the flurries of snow to their lodging. They had been invited to dine with the Washingtons and other couples. Hannah was glad to be alone with her officer again; the evening meal and discussions had been pleasant and not extravagant, but she could not forget her worries and the day's conversations.

They entered their cabin; Ezekiel raked the embers and built up the fire. He stood and sighed heavily. Hannah went to him, asking, "What's wrong?"

"You told me you took food and medicine to some of my men, and you ask what's wrong? You are not blind, Hannah," he replied bitterly.

"No, I'm not. I've seen the despair, the questioning, the confusion, the hardships. But I've also seen men who still cling to their hope and faith."

"Lucky fools!" Ezekiel muttered, pacing the short space between the walls.

"Why do you call them fools for still hoping and believing?" Hannah asked, surprised to hear the challenge ringing in her tone.

Ezekiel turned, responding with angry fierceness. "Because! Because I've seen our patriot's dream falter and die this year. We have no support from Congress. The troops are starving and deserting. I can't even keep my unit together. We lost the capital. It's over. It's only a matter of time until we are crushed. And then what? Hanging, imprisonment, exile..."

"Stop," Hannah cried. "Please stop." She swallowed the lump in her throat. Now wasn't a time for tears. Courage was needed. "Patriot dreams do not die. The odds may be against us, but has God ever failed us when we have called upon His name? Again and again, I have seen Him give victory when we have humbled ourselves. Gideon had three hundred men, but he defeated a mighty army because of his faith in God."

Ezekiel made an impatient gesture. "Faith. Yes,

Hannah, I know. I have faith in God. I've seen the victories, but now..."

Hannah put her hands on her husband's shoulders. "Now, you are doubting. Faith can move mountains, build armies, win wars, but you must have faith that He will do it in His perfect time. You cannot let pride stand in your way. As the Bible reminds us, stand still, take courage, wait upon the Lord."

He bent his head toward her, resting his cheek on her linen cap. "But why the trial?" Ezekiel murmured.

"Trials are God's way of making us strong, building faith, humbling pride," Hannah responded, embracing him. "Perhaps we were too proud from victories. Too trusting in our own strength. Is this winter of hardship to forge the men and leaders a new nation must have?"

Ezekiel groaned softly. "Pride, Hannah. I struggle. I don't know if I can conquer it."

Hours later, Hannah shivered in her nest of blankets and felt someone kiss her cheek. "You must see this sunrise, dearest," Ezekiel whispered. After straightening her clothes and finding a cape, she opened the door and stepped into the early light of dawn. "I went walking," Ezekiel said, wrapping his arms around her. "I couldn't sleep, and I was thinking about what you said. We can't win this fight on our own. I pray God will favor our cause. If we are victorious, it will be because of hard work and His blessing." He whispered close to her ear. "I'm sorry that I was giving up. Thank you for reminding me what's important."

The eastern sky glowed with a pale golden light. "The darkest night can become the brightest day.

Maybe this winter is our country's hour before dawn." Hannah nodded and wiped away the happy tears. Her soldier had won and was again a determined patriot commander. She looked up at him, thrilling at his quiet smile and confident expression.

Someone cleared their throat nearby, and Ezekiel released Hannah, both of them glancing around. Private Isaac Hammond stood by the corner of the cabin with a stack of wood in his arms. "Sorry. I was just going to leave it by the door," he said.

"Thank you," Ezekiel replied, while Hannah asked quietly, "You're still here?"

"Yeah." Private Hammond kicked at a pile of snow. "I was thinking about what you said about heroes. Decided I had to stay. After-all, there's a rumor that the French are comin' and some fellow who knows how to teach drill and make us real soldiers. Figured I'd stay a little longer..."

"I'm glad," Hannah answered. Ezekiel squeezed her hand.

"I'd best be goin'," the soldier said, saluting and disappearing around the cabin corner.

Together, Hannah and Ezekiel stood watching the dismal scene of yesterday transform to a picturesque moment of beauty as the new sunlight made the snow glisten. "It will still be a long road to victory," Hannah whispered.

"Yes," Ezekiel replied, putting his arm around her shoulders. "But patriot dreams don't die. Rather, they become the visions for the future. A future when our flag will wave in the land, and we will be free."

EAST TO WEST

1838

TRAIL OF TEARS

EAST TO WEST

"They were searching for a King," John murmured, pulling his worn blanket closer as a biting wind whipped through the camp. Hesitatingly, he pushed his bare hand into the cold to toss more broken sticks on the faltering fire.

Beside him, Grandfather shifted, his hoarse voice asking in the Cherokee language, "Did you say something?"

"It doesn't matter," John replied. "Are you alright?"

Grandfather nodded. "Cold. But a warrior shouldn't complain."

"I can't remember a colder winter in my fifteen years."

"It's because we're farther north. Far from home," Grandfather sighed.

Around them, men, women, and children of the Cherokee Nation huddled, trying not to grumble and forcing back their freezing tears. Yards away, the soldiers laughed with holiday mirth. Laughter, cruel slurs, pity, sincere apologies – they'd heard it all as the sun rose and set, and the moon signaled the long, passing months. In the summer, the news had come to their farms in North Georgia: evacuation. Years of petition and court cases had failed. The white men – searching for gold and seeking prosperous farms – wanted their land. It hadn't mattered that these first native peoples of America were well-established, running orderly communities, and had adopted many of the white man's customs through the direction of missionaries.

John rubbed his cold hands. And it hadn't mattered that many had white man's blood in their veins. His mother had married a missionary's son – a good man who had died when John was eight, leaving three children and a grieving widow. That's when Grandfather had come, arriving from the deep forest to take his place with the family.

Grandfather came with his stories and legends, his traditional skills and craftsmanship, and his skepticism of the "white man's faith." Mother was patient; uncompromising in her beliefs and her commitment that her children would go to church and read the Bible. When Grandfather scoffed, Mother prayed. "Someday," she said with beautiful confidence, "he will ask, and we will tell him about Jesus."

The years had passed with poor and bountiful harvests; they had managed, until this summer when the soldiers came. The forced march away from their home to the disease-ridden fort had bewildered John. It angered his Grandfather. "I saw this Andrew Jackson. Fought for him. And now he has allowed them to make us leave our homeland. I would fight him and the other

American chiefs. I would die. But I must think of my family and the others. Still, I search for a leader."

There was no leader in the snowy camp that night, only the remnants of a proud nation and the rough guards and guides, leading them west. Beside John, Grandfather slapped his hands together with a quick, violent gesture. "What are they singing, John?" He stared at the silhouetted soldiers.

"It's Christmas, Grandfather. You remember? When Mother and us children would go to church to celebrate when Jesus came to earth as a baby."

"I remember. That Man you call Jesus."

John nodded, and Grandfather asked, "You want to be celebrating this day with them?"

"No, not with the soldiers," John replied softly in his native language. Grandfather seemed satisfied.

Lying back, John began tracing the patterns in the starry sky. The wise men who traveled to Bethlehem to find Jesus had followed a star. There would be no King at the end of this trek to the Great Plains – just his mother and sisters who'd been sent west in another group earlier in the year. They would be waiting, if they weren't already buried along the trail. The stars and faith were the only similarities between this night and the one thousands of years ago.

"I've told you our peoples' legends about the stars?" Grandfather questioned.

"Yes."

"Did your father's people have stories about the stars?"

"Yes. There was this one star..." John paused. Grandfather did not like to talk about white men and their ways anymore. For a while, he had tried to understand, but, after the last frustrating months, he had stopped asking questions. Until now.

"Go on," Grandfather urged. "I think of the stories I know. I hum our peoples' songs. They are part of us, but tonight it only makes me sad. Makes me remember all we are losing. Tell me something different?"

For a moment, John was confused. Then he remembered his mother's words that someday Grandfather would ask and they would tell him the truth. Was this the day? Taking a deep breath, John began, "Once there were wise men, living in the east. They studied and watched the stars. One night, they saw a new star appear. They searched in their books and in their stories to see what it meant."

"Was it war?" He clutched his blanket as though longing for a weapon.

"No, no, Grandfather. Much better. It meant that a leader had been born. A promised King. They gathered gifts and journeyed to find him." The verses John had read so many times to his mother on Christmas Eve came easily to his recollection. " '*When they saw the star, they rejoiced with exceedingly great joy. And when they had come into the house, they saw the young Child with Mary his mother, and fell down and worshipped him. And when they had opened their treasures, they presented gifts to Him: gold, frankincense, and myrrh.*' "

"A sign for a leader," Grandfather whispered. "What kind of leader was he?"

The verse from the prophet Isaiah echoed in

John's mind. "He was Wonderful. A Counselor. Mighty God. Everlasting Father. Prince of Peace. And His nation will last forever."

"A great Chief. Not like these we have now. Oh, that I could meet such a leader!"

Slowly, explaining the best way he knew, John told Grandfather about Jesus – His attributes, His redemption, and His everlasting tribe, gathered from every group of people. Grandfather nodded, listening wordlessly. "Sleep now," he ordered gently, when John paused wondering what to say next. "You must have strength. I will think about what you have said." Closing his eyes, John silently prayed and eventually slept, though the cold penetrated through the blankets and woolen clothes.

He woke when Grandfather shook his shoulder. "The last stars are almost gone. Soon we will be going." John sat up, rubbing his eyes and finger-combing his dark hair. "Look quickly," Grandfather ordered. "Before the stars are gone, I must tell you something."

The sky was deep winter blue with a faint glow toward the east. Above, the brightest stars still glittered. "I see them, Grandfather," John said.

"I have found Him," Grandfather said. "The Leader. Last night I finally understood what you believe about one God – Jesus. I won't follow anyone else now. Only Him. You will have to explain many things to me, but I will be His warrior."

The soldiers were calling the people to stand and prepare for the day's journey. Grandfather and John moved toward the front of the line. "I am still a Cherokee. But I finally realize that, whether my culture and nation survives or not, I have a leader who lives and who will not leave me."

John smiled. He could not wait to see his mother and tell her what had happened. One brilliant star lingered in the lightening sky, like a rejoicing, guiding beacon. "I see a star," Grandfather said.

"And we will rejoice with exceedingly great joy," John added. Miles and miles of snow and ice lay ahead of them on this forced journey from east to west, but there – along the way – Grandfather had found the King, and every night the stars would remind them of God's promises and miracles.

A LIGHT IN THE WINDOW

1848

CALIFORNIA

Sarah Kay Bierle

A LIGHT IN THE WINDOW

Charles Henderson was coming back. The thought troubled Barbara all through the evening, making it difficult to focus as she helped her younger sister finish the Christmas decorations. Five-year-old Margarite laughed at Barbara's distracted attempts to finish the long paper chains to hang around the windows. Anytime, Charles Henderson would return; he had promised to come on Christmas Eve or Christmas Day. "Put a candle in the front window, if you want me to ask again," he had instructed her six weeks earlier as he set out on his journey to San Francisco to see his sick brother.

Abuela (grandmother) hummed a Christmas tune as she tied the freshly cut pepper tree sprigs into a small garland to lay on the mantle. When the final touches were complete, she lit the candles in her silver candlesticks, smiling at the Margarite's enthusiasm. Barbara twirled her little sister around the room, both of them giggling as they collapsed on the worn sofa.

"Tell me a story," Margarite begged. Barbara

forced herself out of her confused dreamland and told holiday stories. As the evening grew later, Abuela said good-night and retired to her room. Margarite begged for one more story, and Barbara agreed.

However, Margarite couldn't keep her eyes open and fell asleep, leaving Barbara to admire the enchanting image of her little sister curled on the sofa, waiting for Christmas. In a few hours, she would awaken and clamor for her gifts with happy excitement. Barbara smiled faintly; the gifts would be few this year, but she and Abuela had tried to fashion some little toys. There was nothing for Barbara to look forward to – except the ride to church for the service and the pleasure of seeing her brothers after their two day stay at a neighboring rancho.

What will you do? Barbara asked herself, as she glanced at the curtains and dark windows before gently picking up Margarite. It's alright, she told herself, walking to the girls' bedroom. You don't need to be anxious. Mr. Henderson will...? There her thoughts stopped, and she tucked her sleeping sister into bed. What will he do? Why did she sense he could help her, just by sharing the burden of caring for the family and trying to hold on to the rancho? "He's mercenary," she whispered, closing the bedroom door and trying to make her head overrule the longing in her heart. "He's only looking to make his fortune and, for some reason, thinks he can do it here."

Shaking her head, Barbara leaned against the adobe wall in the shadowy courtyard. The dry leaves from the vines rattled along the hard-packed dirt paths, and the fountain trickled eerily in the chilly California night. It would never have come to this way if Abuelo (grandfather) and Papa were still alive. Angrily, Barbara walked down the corridor, her heeled shoes echoing hollowly. How dare Charles Henderson try to profit from their misfortune!

She went to the sitting room and picked at her embroidery, blinking rapidly in an attempt to keep the tears from falling. Everything had gone wrong. Tragedy had followed Barbara's life for five years. Her Mama had died after Margarite was born. The next year Papa's beautiful house in Monterey had caught fire and burned to the ground, forcing them to leave the whirling, exciting society to live on the family rancho with his parents. After that, Abuelo – who had always treasured and looked after Barbara and her siblings – died of fever. Then it was 1846; Papa had gone to fight the Americanos who were trying to take over Alta California. Just before Christmas, he had died of wounds. And, in 1847, the creditors came. The rancho had not been as productive as it could've been, and it was hard to pay the debts. Most of the cattle were taken, stripping the rancho of its livelihood. Somehow, the proud family had survived – scrimping, saving, pretending.

Abuela had decided the younger children – Alfonso, Juan, and Margarite – must have schooling. In the summer, she had brought an itinerate schoolteacher to the rancho, allowing him to educate her grandchildren in return for food and a room. "We must not be ignorant," Abuela had insisted. "Barbara, you were well-educated by a governess. Your siblings must have the same opportunity, even if you and I must do without pretty dresses to pay for the extra food."

Barbara had protested fiercely. "I agree that education is important, but please, Abuela – do not have them taught by an Americano. No! Papa was killed fighting against them. This man has said he was a soldier before he mustered out. He fought at the battle where Papa was shot."

"And who else can you find who will teach three children at a lonely rancho for nothing more than room and board?" Abuela argued. Barbara had yielded, but had expected the worst from the Americano schoolteacher. However, expectations are not always reality.

She tossed her embroidery back into the work basket and looked at the meager holiday decorations. It was nothing like the days of her childhood. Just the paper chains and pepper tree greenery and berries trying to replace the long, beautiful garlands and yards of ribbon from years gone by. A bowl of softening fruit stood on the sideboard accented with juniper while the fruit flies swarmed around it during the day. Abuela's silver candlesticks – brought from Mexico and treasured for generations – lined the mantle, burning toward their last glow of the evening. Barbara leaned her head on her hands, frowning.

Last summer, frowning hadn't done her any good. No matter how many cool words, sweeping exits, or hostile glares she had shot at Charles Henderson, the schoolmaster did not seem to take her hints. He had still greeted her every morning, brought her flowers from the garden once a week, escorted her to her chair in the dining room like a true gentleman, and helped her with arithmetic when she had pounded the record books in desperate frustration. By autumn, she found his conversation delightfully interesting, and it was hard to throw his flowers out the window, but she could not forget his nationality. His accent was rough, and sometimes he haltingly searched for the correct Spanish word. He was good-looking in a New England way – fair skinned with curly brown hair and a short mustache. His smile was quite unforgettable. And then he asked her to marry him, offering to stay at the rancho and help the family recover. He had ideas – plans – to make the rancho successful again. But Barbara resented charity and shook her head. Seeing that she was unwilling, he had offered to come back after his trip. At that point in the conversation, Barbara had felt overwhelmingly confused and had darted away.

He will be coming soon, she thought as she watched the candle flames cast shadows on the adobe walls. Oh, what shall I do? He could've wounded my father. Can I think that of a husband every time I look at him? No!

"Senorita Barbara," whispered Maria, the devoted servant, as she peered in at the door. "Senora Esparanza would like to see you."

"Tell Abuela I will come at once," Barbara replied, rising from her low seat and shaking the floor dust from the hem of her gown.

Abuela was in bed, looking warm and content in her flannel nightgown and lacy cap. "Nieta! (granddaughter) Darling!" She laid aside the book she had been reading. "Feliz Navidad, almost. (Happy Christmas)." She laughed at her own joke, then sobered. "Why the tears, Barbara? Everything will be well, I promise."

Barbara sat on the stool close to the bed and buried her face in the sheets. "I don't know if I love him. I don't know if I could..."

Abuela stroked Barbara's hair. "Love, Nieta? Who?"

"Mr. Henderson asked me to marry him. I am supposed to let him know when he returns tonight or tomorrow."

"And why would you say no?"

"Why?" Barbara exclaimed, looking at her grandmother. "He's an Americano. It is hard to forgive them for Papa's death. Now, they have taken over California. And you have let one of them into our household! I don't want one to steal my heart. You would not want that, would you?"

"Barbara, Barbara. If he was not an Americano, would you say yes?"

"But he is..." she started to reply, then stopped, seeing Abuela's searching look. "Yes," she murmured with a blush.

"He is a good man. He told me he was sick during the battle. He did not fight, and I believe him." Abuela pulled the blanket higher and shifted comfortably on her pillows. "Someday, you must learn to forgive, Barbara. Let the hurt and grief of the past go." She looked at the religious image hanging on the wall across from her bed. "Christ came as a babe. To live and to die, to make a way for forgiveness from God. How can you go pray in church tomorrow morning? How can you expect God to forgive you, if you cannot forgive others?"

"So if I could...forgive him...you would not be angry if I accepted his offer of marriage?"

"No, darling. I would be happy for you. And remember, he would not steal your heart if you gave it willingly. Think on it." Abuela clapped her hands together. "Now, now, off to bed or at least let me sleep. Buenos Noche, mi Nieta Barbara. (Good night, my Granddaughter Barbara.)"

Barbara closed the door softly. "He wasn't there," she murmured. Closing her eyes, she could imagine Mr. Henderson's smile. Barbara caught her breath as the faint sound of hoof beats pounded up the dirt road. "God, help me. Forgive me for my bitterness. Let me be thankful for a blessing and open my heart."

Feeling free, she ran toward the sitting room. There was no candle in the front window. What would he think? Would he turn his horse and gallop away without seeing her?

On the mantle, one last candle burned. She touched the silver holder, feeling the fine craftsmanship of her ancestors' homeland. "I forgive," she whispered. Grasping it firmly and taking a deep breath, she walked to the window. Can he still love me? she wondered. Maybe he has changed his mind? Deep inside, she knew she didn't want that.

Holding the silver candlestick, Barbara drew back the curtain. Outside, Mr. Henderson stood by his horse, staring at the dark home with a forlorn expression. He looked at her with questioning eyes. She knew at that moment she always wanted to make him smile.

"Love given willingly from a heart that has known forgiveness," Barbara whispered. She nodded a silent reply to his wordless question and beamed a brilliant welcoming look. Then he smiled too.

Sarah Kay Bierle

THE CHRISTMAS SERMON

1862

CIVIL WAR

Sarah Kay Bierle

THE CHRISTMAS SERMON

The glow of dawn slid over the city, silhouetting the church steeples and snow covered roofs. Christmas morning. The light grew stronger, gently illuminating a sickroom on the second floor of a Union hospital. The patient in the tiny room, shifted, moaned, and opened his eyes. Daniel, the young chaplain at the bedside, breathed a sigh of relief. "It's morning," he said.

The sick man smiled wanly. "I survived?"

"You survived," Daniel replied, running his hand over the leather cover of the Bible. His night of wakeful prayer was over.

He held a cup of water to the sick man's dry lips, then stood, raised the invalid higher on the pillows, and smoothed the bed quilt. It had not been what he expected last night – arriving late after a day's long train ride. Met by his older brother – Surgeon Frederick Martin – and asked to sit up with a gasping soldier. In the dark hours, he wondered what he had expected when he volunteered as a chaplain with the United States Christian Commission. Completing theological school, but having no church of his own, Daniel had decided to preach to the army. He subconsciously patted his pocket where he had placed the notes for his first Christmas sermon.

He'd always imagined he would preach his first holiday message in a small wooden church, lavishly decorated with pine, holly, boxwood, and gold ribbons. The congregation, in their winter finest, would listen with rapt attention to every word; the feathers on the ladies' Christmas bonnets would bob as they nodded their agreement, and the gentlemen would enthusiastically say "amen." And, perhaps, if he was very lucky, there would be a young lady with unforgettably bright eyes, and he'd know she was the girl he was going to court and marry in the coming year... Though, Daniel had only been at the hospital a few hours, he already knew he wouldn't preach his first Christmas message in that picturesque little chapel and probably wouldn't meet that charming little lady, but he still anticipated sharing and encouraging the soldiers.

"Daniel?" questioned his older brother, pushing open the half-closed door. "Ah, Private Fletcher," he continued, entering and seeing the soldier awake, "good to see you up." He reached for the patient's wrist and counted his pulse, then felt his forehead. "Fever's broke. You need to eat and sleep, but I am confident you'll stay in the land of the living for a while yet."

"Thanks, Doc."

"Daniel, will you go get some food for Mr. Fletcher and assist him if necessary?" Nodding and promising to return, Daniel followed his brother out of the room.

On the stair landing Frederick stopped, turned, and embraced his brother. "Thanks, Dan. I didn't have time to tell you last night. I'm glad you're here." Frederick let his brother go and asked, "Are you alright? I threw you into the fray rather quickly."

"It's not what I expected." Daniel replied, shrugging. "I'm fine. A little tired..."

"Coffee cures that around here," Frederick promised. "Now, I have to be on my morning rounds. We'll talk later."

"When do you want me to preach the sermon?" Daniel asked, then frowned at his brother's astonished look. "It is Christmas Day, you know."

"If you can find time and a willing congregation within these walls, go ahead and preach your sermon whenever you want. First, get some food for that hungry man." Frederick nodded abruptly and started up the stairs to the third floor.

Taking a deep breath to suppress his irritation with his brother's attitude, Daniel smiled, "Um, Frederick? Where's the kitchen?"

With a grin at his own forgetfulness, Frederick pointed the way downstairs. A few minutes later, Daniel was back at Private Fletcher's bedside, and, while the invalid slowly ate, they talked a little. The young soldier wasn't interested in religion, but his smile brightened when Daniel offered to write a letter home for him. Private Fletcher struggled to stay awake as he dictated the final words, and Daniel left quietly. Now would be a good time to share his Christmas message. As he climbed to the third floor, he reviewed his topic: why Christ came to earth. His outline was filled with numerous Scripture verses and deep theological points, true credit to his academic training.

The third floor was an open attic. Five men lay on cots. The chaplain inwardly grimaced at the bloody bandages which concealed the worst of the painful wounds, but the soldiers kept up a lively chatter about how the barren room needed holiday cheer. "No fault of the doctors or nurses," one man commented in Irish brogue. "They are so busy."

"Who are you? And what are you doing here?" another fellow with a bushy red beard asked.

"I...I'm a chaplain. Would you like to hear a sermon?" Their stares answered his question. Daniel tugged at his shirt collar and cravat. They wanted Christmas that they could see – not hear – he thought dejectedly. "I might be able to find something. To decorate the room."

"Could you?" chorused the weary voices. Promising to be back soon, Daniel descended to the lowest level and stepped into the cold, snowy yard. A boxwood hedge and a prickly holly bush. It would do. Using his pocket-knife, he cut some boughs and headed inside, snatching a white bandage from a table.

While the men sang with jolly gusto, Daniel tied the greenery and hung it around the room. "Thanks, Chaplain. That sure made the day better," they called.

Now for the sermon, Daniel thought, wondering if he would find more willing listeners on the first floor. "Oh, thank goodness," a harried orderly exclaimed. "Come help us, Chaplain. It's dinnertime, and we can always use help distributing the food." For the next hour, Daniel was too busy to even think about his holiday message. Scurrying up and down the stairs, he carried trays of steaming soup and fresh bread, and then returned the empty dishes to the kitchen again. His stomach growled, but apparently now wasn't the time for the staff and assistants to eat.

"Chaplain, Chaplain," called a weary woman. "I don't have a clue what to do with these folks, but we can't leave them in the cold snow. Please help." The nurse pointed to the front hall, then dashed upstairs with a basin of water while somewhere up above Frederick urged her to hurry.

In the doorway to the hall, Daniel stopped. A family – father, mother, twin boys, young girl, and a toddler – huddled together. "Is we free now?" one of the boys questioned, tugging at his mother's ragged skirt.

"Please, sir," the man said, "we've run from our master and is tryin' to find freedom. We saw those men in uniform. Are we safe now?"

"You are free," Daniel said with a welcoming smile, extending his hand.

"Where do we go now? What do we do?" the woman asked, her dark face frowning with worry as she looked at her shivering children.

"The kitchen," Daniel replied. "Let's find you some food and a warm place to sit. Then I'll help you decide what to do next.

The cooks put their hands in the air as Daniel entered with the family. "Just for a few moments," he bargained.

"Fine," snapped the busy matron. "But I don't have extra food. Just what's there on the table for the assistants."

Daniel's stomach growled, but he saw the weariness and fright on the children's faces.

They've come so far, he thought. So far to run for freedom. He picked up two large bowls of soup and some bread. "It's not much," he admitted. "But it's what we can spare."

"God bless you," the woman said, with tears in her eyes while her husband shook Daniel's hand again.

While the family ate, Daniel went out, made inquiries, and, after hours of tramping along the icy street, found the home of a family who worked on the Underground Railroad. They agreed to look after the family for a couple days until the man could find work and a place to live. Daniel led the family to the welcoming home, carrying one of the children in his arms.

The light of the short winter day was fading as he wearily walked back through the snowy streets. He marveled at the beauty of the scene, the pure loveliness of the snow and the wonder of the gently falling flakes. How strongly it contrasted with the hurried crimson scenes in the hospital wards.

Humming a carol and still hoping to preach his sermon, Daniel pushed open the front door of the hospital and entered chaos. Two orderlies hurried by, carrying a man on a stretcher. His brother rushed after them while a nurse ran the other direction, calling for warm water. "What's happening?" he questioned, not realizing he spoke aloud until the hustling assistant surgeon replied. "Excessive bleeding. Infection. A secondary amputation's needed to save the man's life."

Daniel's stomach twisted at the sound of the frightened soldier's piteous cries. "Don't let me die. Don't let me die." He pressed against the wall, trying to steady his unsettled stomach. Around the corner in the operating room, he heard someone fall to the ground. "Get that nurse out of here. We'll take care of her later." He heard the panic and frustration in his brother's voice. "We need some help in here. Halloo – anyone?"

Pushing away from the wall, Daniel walked to the doorway. "I...I'm here. Do you need me?"

"Fine. Don't faint," Frederick responded. "Hand me the instruments. Just like the hours you helped me study at home. Only this time, there's blood."

Later, Daniel stumbled out the back door and sat on the steps. He felt shaken by the surgery scene. "And I never got to preach my sermon," he thought.

The door opened, and Frederick joined him, pushing a cup of hot coffee into his hands. "Thanks for assisting. You probably helped us save that man's life."

"Will the nurse be alright?"

"Yes, she's worn out. Rest and proper food will help. She works too hard, but there aren't enough orderlies, nurses, or assistants. Ever." Frederick leaned back and watched the clouds in the clearing sky. "I'll bet this wasn't what you thought you were signing up for. Was it?"

Daniel shook his head.

"Are you leaving in the morning?"

"No," Daniel replied. "I'll stay, I guess."

"Good. You're needed here," Frederick said, thumping him on the shoulder. "I'm off to the back room to get some sleep. Happy Christmas?"

"Happy Christmas," Daniel repeated glumly. "I never did get to preach my sermon."

Frederick paused in the doorway. "You're wrong, Dan. You preached a better, stronger sermon than every other chaplain who's wandered in and out of here in the last six months." He closed the door, leaving Daniel wondering.

Slowly, he pulled the sermon notes from his pocket. One copied verse in his outline caught his eye: a prophecy about Christ's role in His first coming.

The Spirit of the Lord God is on Me; because the Lord has anointed Me to preach good tidings to the meek; He has sent me to bind up the brokenhearted, to proclaim liberty to the captives, and the opening of the prison to them that are bound.

Be like Christ, he thought. Isn't that the goal of every minister? Perhaps actions are louder than words. Kindness more eloquent than fine speech. Perseverance more lasting than rhetoric.

Daniel squared his shoulders. "I'll stay," he whispered to the empty back lot. "Someday, I'll preach a sermon or have time to read and pray with the soldiers. But until then, I'll remember what I learned this Christmas. Service before sermons. Perhaps that is the most effective way to share my faith."

<u>CURSES OR BLESSINGS?</u>

1870'S

THE GILDED AGE

CURSES OR BLESSINGS?

Young Molly O'Bryan stirred the thin soup and motioned her five younger siblings to be quiet. Now, wasn't the time to sing Christmas carols. Mama was resting, and she needed all her strength. Molly glanced nervously toward the bedroom; the midwife, who lived in an apartment two floors above, had come today and said Mama had to be careful or the baby might come too early.

The door opened, and Father entered, tossed his cap on the peg, and stomped dejectedly to the table. "Hard day at work?" Molly asked, as he sat down in one of the creaky chairs.

"Lost me job," he groaned. "But I stayed 'way from the pub to keep me promise to yer mother. Curse 'o the Hamiltons again."

"Hopefully you can find another soon," Molly replied, beckoning the children to the table and setting out the bowls and spoons. She didn't need to ask what he meant about the curse; anytime something went wrong, Father blamed the English family who had caused hardship and tragedy for the O'Bryan clan in Ireland.

"We'll talk. Where's yer mother?"

"Resting. Can we talk later?" She looked at the children, hinting that perhaps it was something little ears shouldn't hear.

"What's it, Molly dear?" Father asked, when they were sitting alone at the table while Eric, Thomas, Patrick, Kate, and Bess played with their blocks in the corner.

Slowly, Molly explained what the midwife had said and her concern about Mama. "If all doesn't go well, there may be doctor's bills," she added.

"And we were just beginnin' to have a 'ittle savings," Father lamented, running his hands through his hair. "And now, no job. Whatever will we do? With no job, me savings will 'ave to go for the rent and food."

"Leaving nothing for the doctor, if Mama needs help." Molly leaned her chin on her hands and said earnestly, "I've been thinking, Father. I can work. Eric is nine – old enough to mind the others."

"No, dear." Father reached for Molly's hand. "I need ye here."

"But, Father, I'm almost fifteen. I could get a job as a maid. I'm good at housework and looking after children. It would ease our situation and bring some extra money."

Father tapped the table to emphasize his words. "Absolutely not. I don't want ye working in a rich 'ouse until ye are older and wiser."

"If it was a good family? Would you let me? Peter and Will are working and boarding elsewhere already, and they are younger than me."

"They're boys. Don't worry, Molly dear. I'll find

work t'morrow."

Four tomorrows came and went. The rent on the tiny apartment came due, leaving little money in the hidden jar. Mama continued to rest, but the midwife shook her head again.

"Father, we must do something," Molly urged. "You know I don't want to leave, but there seems little other option. Neighbor Ryan loaned me his week-old newspaper, and I've been reading the advertisements. There's one family in a very good part of the city. They need a maid. It would pay well, and I think I could do the work. I'd have to stay there, but I could come home one day of the week."

Father shook his head. "I don't want ye to go. But I don't know what else we can do."

"If we don't do something to make money, they will turn us out next month. January. Winter. And where will we find lodging then? Please, Father, think about it."

He hesitated, searching for another way. Wearily, he rubbed his eyes. "Alright. Tell me the 'ouse address." Father sighed after Molly told him the location. "It seems we have no other way. If the job is still there – 'member the paper is a week old – ye can apply for it. But only until I have a job of me own. Then ye'll quit. Understand?" Molly nodded.

The following day Molly clutched the iron fence and stared up at the large city home with its elegant trim and shutters. What a different place – almost a different world – compared to her family's bare, crowded apartment where holidays were hardly celebrated. At least not celebrated the way the rich folks did. At this grand mansion,

Christmas wreaths hung on the double doors, and garland had been twined on the bannister bordering the steps to the front door. Shyly, she pushed open the gate and went to the side entrance – the servants' door – and knocked. "I have to do this," she told herself.

A tall Irish woman with a cheery smile opened the door, wiping her hands on her apron. "May I 'elp you?"

"I was wondering..." Molly paused, trying to stop the fluttering, nervous feeling in her chest. "I was wondering if the serving girl's position was still open at this house?"

" 'Tis. The girl who came first was an utter failure, but you look like a smart lass. Come in and meet the housekeeper."

Mrs. Rorke, the housekeeper, sternly looked Molly up and down before announcing, "You can have a two day trial. Mr. and Mrs. Hamilton are good society people and must keep up a respectable establishment. It is my job to see that the household runs properly, so I will decide if you stay or go."

Molly nodded. "Did you say the family's name was Hamilton?"

"Yes, I did." Mrs. Rorke peered over her spectacles. "Does that concern you?"

"No," Molly managed to say, unwilling to lose the opportunity for work. Ten minutes later as she started ironing the linen napkins, her hands shook. Hamiltons! She shuddered as she remembered Father's stories about the "Hamilton Curse."

Molly had grown up hearing stories about a family with that surname in Ireland. Father could remember the Great Famine and had instilled a firm mistrust of all Englishmen and Hamiltons in his children's minds. Hamiltons had let their Irish neighbors starve. Hamiltons had taken part in the conviction and hanging of Uncle Thomas for supposed revolutionary actions. The family had escaped the Hamiltons and taken passage for America, hoping to flee famine and oppression. Hamiltons were the curse of the O'Bryan family – at least in Father's stories. Superstitiously, Molly feared that some evil would befall her family since she had entered this house. Was the money she would be paid cursed?

Then reason began to conquer her imagination. It would be very unlikely these were the same Hamiltons. Everything would be fine. This was America, not Ireland. She was just a servant. But she would try to prevent Father from finding out the family's surname. Quitting a job because of a name seemed ridiculous, especially when they needed money.

The following day as Molly ran up and down stairs, helping lay out the tea things, setting the dining table, and learning to answer the bells from different rooms to inquire what was needed, she caught glimpses of the rich family. Mr. and Mrs. Hamilton seemed like pleasant folks. Young Mr. Hamilton was home on Christmas holidays from college while Miss Hamilton's laughter and music brightened the home. They did not seem dangerous or unkind.

The house amazed Molly. Every time she climbed the stairs from the basement or entered the hall from the kitchen, she felt like she entered a wonderland. Plush carpets covered the floors and the walls were decorated with gilded wallpaper. The ornate furniture and abundance of knick-knacks were endless curiosities to a young lady who was accustomed to plain, useful, and cheap. Best of all were the Christmas decorations. Gold, silver, and burgundy ribbons held boughs and sprigs of greenery to the stair railings. Mistletoe hung from the chandeliers, and garlands of holly perched on the large mirrors in the hallway and parlor. Molly was convinced she could've bought her family's food for a month with the amount of money that must have been spent on decorations, but she still admired the beautiful, impractical holiday trimmings.

On the second evening, Mrs. Rorke told Molly she had passed the tests and had the job. Breathing an inward sigh of relief, Molly thanked her. The work would be hard, and it would be challenging to only see her family one day per week, but Molly was relieved to know Mama, Father, and the children would at least have safe and warm shelter through the winter months. Lying in her attic bed, she prayed that Mama and the baby were alright. Curling under the warm blanket, she tried to ignore her anxiety and loneliness.

The next morning as she carried out a bucket of ashes, Molly saw Father waiting by the back gate. "It ain't the same at home without ye, Molly. But since I hain't found work, I'm glad o' this for a time. Yer a good 'aughter, Molly dear," he said, kissing her on the forehead. "Yer alright?"

"Yes. The other servants are kind, and the family is good, I think. How's Mama?"

"No better. No worse. I'll send for ye, if anything

happens and ye need to come. And ye come right home if anything..."

"Yes, Father. Take care of Mama," Molly whispered, fighting back her tears. It would not be easy, these days away from home and kindred.

Someone approached. "Letter fer Miss Hamilton. Miss Baldwin said not to wait fer a reply." Molly took the letter and nodded to the other servant.

"Hamilton?" Father questioned, frowning fiercely.

"Molly, Molly. Don't dawdle. You're needed in the kitchen at once," Mrs. Rorke called from the pantry window.

"Hamilton?" Father repeated.

"I can explain next time," Molly insisted. "I have to go. I have to keep this job. Forgive me." She ran toward the door, afraid to look back, afraid to see the hurt and confused expression on Father's face.

The following day Molly trudged upstairs to Miss Hamilton's dressing room, carrying two elegant gowns she had finished pressing. After tapping on the door, she entered and saw the young lady lounging on a low sofa, reading a fashion magazine. "Your dresses, Miss. Shall I hang them in the wardrobe?"

"Yes, thank you," Miss Hamilton answered. "Forgive me if I'm prying, but what do you and your family do for Christmas?"

"Be together, if we can. Go to church, if we can. We usually sing the holiday songs from our country," Molly replied simply.

"You don't have any special traditions?"

"Not really. It's not a fancy day for us. Usually we're not all together. Someone has work. There's not enough money for a feast or gifts. It's a gift just to see everyone. Father's jobs are often away from us, and two of my brothers board and work at a factory on the other side of the city. And, this year, I won't be home."

"Oh?"

Molly blushed, not sure if she could get in trouble with Mrs. Rorke for talking with Miss Hamilton. "My day off won't come until the 27th of December."

"I'm sorry. How different from the way we celebrate," Miss Hamilton mused. "But I wonder if we value being together as much as your family does?" She paused, straightening her lace edged sleeves. "You mentioned songs. My grandfather lived in Ireland and had a large estate there, I'm told."

Molly felt sick and dizzy. Could it be true? Was this the same family? What if Father's stories about the Hamiltons and pursuing misfortune were true?

"Are you well?" Miss Hamilton asked.

Feeling weak, Molly leaned against the door frame, but replied, "Yes. Was there anything else you needed?"

"Please, Molly – that's your name, right? Sit down. You don't look well at all." Miss Hamilton took her by the arm and seated her in a low chair. "Is anything the matter? Don't be afraid."

Molly tried to pull herself together, insisting she was well. She could not tell Miss Hamilton about the probable connection between their families. That Miss Hamilton's grandfather had hanged Father's brother – unjustly, according to Father's story.

It seemed that Molly's silence alarmed Miss

Hamilton though. "I will call Mrs. Rorke. You need to rest."

"No! Please, no," Molly protested, frantically fearing that Mrs. Rorke would dismiss her from work. "I just...I'm worried about my mother. She isn't well."

"Do you want to visit her?" Miss Hamilton asked, kneeling beside Molly.

"I can't, Miss. I need to stay here and work. My family needs me to work."

"I'm sorry, but I think I understand. Take a moment to compose yourself. Everything will be alright. And – don't fear – I won't say anything to my mother or Mrs. Rorke."

During the next days, Molly stared with wide-eyed amazement at the holiday preparations and gatherings at the Hamilton home. Guests paraded in and out. The family went to evening entertainments and parties almost every night. Sleighs drawn by beautiful horses with bells on their collars dashed by on the street. The kitchen overflowed with delicious foods. One day, a real evergreen tree was carried into the parlor, and Mrs. and Miss Hamilton hung glass ornaments, ribbons, and tiny gifts on the branches; that evening they had a party and lit the tiny candles that were clipped to the outer branches.

Standing in the background and ready to pour tea or coffee for the guests, Molly watched with wonder. She had not imagined this way of celebrating, and, for a moment she wished her family was rich. Deep inside, though, she just longed to go home, wanted a hug, pined to see Mama's smile, to hear Father's songs, and hold her siblings' hands. "We don't need riches to be happy," she murmured. "We just need our family."

On Christmas Eve – as carolers trooped in and out of the house with laughter and song – Molly choked back tears and tried to focus on her work. She reminded herself that it was just two more days until she could go home. Father had not sent any word, and Molly tried to believe that Mama was better. As she poured tea for a guest, a loud and very un-genteel knocking sounded on the front door. She heard Frances open the door and Eric's unmistakable voice called, "Molly, Molly!"

She set down the tea pot, bobbed a curtsy to the startled family and company, and darted into the hallway. Eric grabbed her hand. "You have to come. It's Mama!"

Forgetting to ask permission, heedless of her superstitions of the Hamilton curse, and only thinking about her beloved parents, Molly ran out the front doors, pulling Eric with her. The city lamps glowed ominously as they rushed through the sleety rain. "What happened?" Molly gasped, as they ran.

"I don't know. But Father came to the bedroom door and said to get you."

By the time they reached the apartment house, Molly realized her panic and flight would probably guarantee that she lost her job. Shaking with grief for Mama and angry at herself for her impulsiveness, she let go of Eric's hand and sprinted up the long flights of stairs. "Am I too late?" she cried, bursting into the apartment.

A baby screamed in the bedroom. Thomas, Patrick, Kate, and Bess huddled on the floor while Peter and Will paced the tiny room. Without answers, they stared at Molly. She crossed the room and pushed open the door. Mama was in bed, and Father sat beside her; the midwife was dressing and soothing a newborn infant. "It's alright, Molly," Father said. Mama smiled weakly. "Just after I sent Eric for ye, everything changed, and the baby was born."

The other children followed Molly into the bedroom, admiring their new baby brother who rested in Mama's arms. Happy tears started in Molly's eyes. Mama was safe, and they were all together. What a blessing! Tomorrow's troubles could be dealt with later. She enjoyed the moment of happiness.

A gentle knock sounded on the door, and, reluctantly, Molly went to answer it. Miss Hamilton and her brother stood there in fur trimmed coats. "I'm dreadfully sorry," Molly whispered. "I shouldn't have run off like I did."

"Never mind," Miss Hamilton replied. "I told my parents and Mrs. Rorke you must have had a particular reason for leaving in a hurry. You had told Frances where you lived, and she recalled. We don't want to intrude, but I wanted to bring this basket of food and tell you that Mrs. Rorke says to take tomorrow with your family and come back to work on the 26th, if you still want to work at our home."

Molly couldn't believe what she heard and stammered her gratitude. "Who's there?" Father asked, coming to the door.

"Miss Hamilton and Mr. Hamilton, Jr.," Molly said quietly. "They bought us this basket. And told me to come back to work day after tomorrow."

"Hamilton, eh?" Father questioned. "From Ireland."

"Our grandfather lived in that country," Mr. Hamilton answered. "I hope that will not be a reason of ill-will."

Father crossed his arms, and Molly touched his shoulder. "If some Hamiltons brought trouble, couldn't others bring blessing?" she whispered. "Isn't it time to let superstition go? Isn't it time to not blame descendants for something they've likely never heard of?"

"I thank ye," Father said, slowly extending his hand. "Will ye step in? Passageway gets chilly."

"We don't want to intrude on your celebrations."

With a genuine grin, Father opened the door wider. "Nonsense. We were just going to sing. Perhaps ye know a carol or two from the old country?"

Miss Hamilton and her brother stood in the bedroom doorway. Father and the children crowded around the bed. Mama smiled happily, holding the baby and looking beautiful with her worn red shawl draped over her nightgown. Father started an old song about preparing for Christmas and considering Christ's coming. All the voices blended in the final verse. O'Bryans and Hamiltons singing together:

If we would then rejoice,
* let's cancel the old score.*
And, purposing amendment,
* resolve to sin no more-*
For mirth can ne'er content us,
* without a conscience clear;*
And thus we'll find true pleasure
* in all the usual cheer,*
In dancing, sport, reveling,

with masquerade and drum.
So let our Christmas merry be,
as Christians doth become.

Sarah Kay Bierle

SONG OF HOPE

1935

THE GREAT DEPRESSION
DUST BOWL

SONG OF HOPE

Mabel hung the twisted circlet of barbed wire decorated with newspaper stars on the door and glanced over her shoulder. There was no black blizzard on the horizon, and she breathed a sigh of relief at the prolonged break from the swirling, choking dust. This year had been hard, so hard. The dust storms had hit the small Texas community without mercy. The crops were non-existent. Poverty was destroying families. Many were leaving – trying to get to California or some other place where there was work and hope. Like Father, the fifteen-year-old thought with a listless shrug.

Seven-year-old Harper Spencer strolled toward the opening in the barbed wire fence. His five-year-old sister – Patty – groped behind him, letting out a soft cry when his exuberant antics separated them. "Children," Mabel called pleasantly, "it's good to see you. Is your mother better today?"

Harper shook his head. "Doc's there. And Pa told us to go out and play."

"Who is it?" Patty asked, reaching out her

hand.

"It's Mabel. Mabel Basset. You remember me, I hope." She knelt down and touched the blind girl gently on the arm.

"Oh, yes. The lady who plays the piano at church."

"When the instrument was clean and not too full of dust," Mabel replied, a touch of sadness in her voice. "Do you want to help me finish our Christmas decorations and stay for lunch?" They nodded. "Well, come in. Mother and I could sure use some friendly company, and we'll rustle up something to eat."

Harper and Patty were often on their own these days. Their mother had given birth and buried a tiny infant; she was still grieving and physically unwell. Their father had started spending most of his time at the saloon down the street. Mabel couldn't bear to see the children looking so sad, hungry, and hopeless; she had invited them home after church last Sunday, and Harper had come over to visit several times since.

"Where's your pa?" Harper asked, as they sat around the table a few minutes later, cutting designs from the holiday cards saved from past years. Already, the children's appearances had improved. Their faces were clean of the smudged dirt, hair brushed, and a missing button in Harper's tattered overalls replaced.

"He's gone west," Mabel's mother replied to the question. "Looking for work. I don't know when he'll be back, or if we'll join him." Her tone was matter-of-fact and didn't invite questions. She helped Patty chain some leftover red yarn, letting her feel the pattern and motions.

"Preacher told us to come to church for Christmas Eve," Patty murmured. "When's that?"

"In five days," Mabel said, holding up a paper star and preparing to string it on the end of Patty's chain.

"There won't be anything for Christmas this year," Harper groaned. "Not even our new baby will be there. Everything's gone."

"And still it's dusty." Patty put down the yarn and started crying.

"But there's always hope," Mabel insisted.

Patty turned her sightless eyes toward Mabel, asking, "What's hope?"

"What's hope?" Mabel repeated, lifting Patty into her lap and drying her tears. "It's what's deep inside you. In your heart. It makes you believe that better days will come. It helps you know that someday we will all laugh and sing and dance and be happy again."

"I don't think anyone has hope 'round here anymore," Harper declared. "They all go to the saloon like my Pa, or they walk around like this." He made a sad, despairing face.

"Maybe we could find a way to help people feel hopeful again. Especially around Christmas time," Mother suggested.

There was silence for a while as they finished their paper and yarn garland. "Music!" Mabel exclaimed. "I'll go ask Pastor Schmidt if we can have a Christmas concert. I could play the piano, and we could all sing carols."

"Piano don't work after the last dust storm," Harper said. "I heard the pastor say that."

"It's alright. Maybe we can clean it. Harper, Patty, do you want to help me? We could make a special –a hopeful – evening for the folks in town."

After lunch and a short walk to church, they were standing in front of the old, battered piano in the sanctuary. Pastor Schmidt had shaken his head skeptically, but agreed to let them try. Together, Mabel and Harper pried open the top and pulled off the front cover. "No strings or hammers broken," Mabel observed.

"It's just dirty, dirty, dirty."

While Patty sat nearby, Harper and Mabel scooped, brushed, wiped, and scrubbed away the layers of dust. Un-tuned sounds reverberated when they pressed the keys, but it was music. Smiling and satisfied, they replaced the protective covers and lid. "Play something, please," Patty whispered.

"We can practice for the concert. What Christmas songs do you know?"

"Don't know any," Harper admitted.

"Oh, then you have to learn a few." Mabel read the words to a couple songs and played the melodies. Harper sang loudly, but Patty shyly refused to try.

"This is wonderful," Pastor Schmidt said, interrupting the musical practice with happy comments and a big grin. "Thank you all for working on our sad piano."

"I can't wait!" Harper told him. "Can I go invite people to our Christmas Eve concert?"

"That would be nice. But why don't you call it a sing-along? That sounds more fun than a concert," the minister suggested. "I'll go up in the attic and see if any of the holiday decorations survived. If you can clean a piano, I can surely brush off some decorations."

"Can I help?" Harper asked, following Pastor Schmidt out the door.

Mabel pressed a few chords on the piano, listening to the grating, un-tuned sounds. Patty touched her sleeve. "Could you teach me?" she whispered. "To play music."

"Well, let's see," Mabel replied, thinking quickly. "I'll lift you onto the piano bench. Can you can reach the keys? There. Do you feel the cool, white ivory keys? Dark black keys are up here." She helped the little girl feel the different key patterns and let her press them to make musical noise.

"Can you help me play a song?" Patty whispered. "For Christmas?"

The pleading look in Patty's empty eyes touched Mabel's heart. So wistful and wanting to hope, but so hesitant that music was yet another pleasure she couldn't enjoy.

"I'm not sure that we have enough time for you to learn a whole song. But maybe we could play one together? Would you like that?"

Patty nodded. Mabel paged through the songbook. Finding the right piece, she placed Patty's small hands on the keys and slowly began teaching the pattern of a single note melody. For the next four days, Mabel led Patty to the church, and they worked on the song. Each day, Patty's smile became brighter, and Mabel rejoiced that she was able to help the little girl.

"I always wanted to make music," Patty said, as they walked back to Mabel's house after the last practice. "Nobody ever thought I could. Thank you for teaching me." She kissed Mabel's hand. "Now, if only my Pa and Ma would come tomorrow to hear."

The next evening Harper and Patty walked to church with Mabel and her mother. "Will they come? What did they say?" Patty asked quietly, tugging on Harper's overalls.

"I don't know, Pat. I hope they come."

"What did they say?" she persisted.

"Nothin'."

The church was brightly lit in the twilight town. As they entered Mabel saw the tinsel and holiday banners and paper flowers. She enthusiastically described the scene to Patty, and the little girl smiled with delight. A few townsfolk had arrived before them and were dusting the layer of grime off the pews.

"I'll play for the sing-along. Then, at the very end, we'll play together," Mabel said, seating Patty on one of the spare chairs near the piano.

Patty nodded. "I remember. That will give Ma and Pa more time to come."

With a sinking feeling, Mabel took her seat at the piano. She didn't know what she would tell Patty if her parents didn't come. She didn't think she could bear the sadness she would see on Patty's face.

When the church was filled with the hearty citizens who wouldn't leave the dusty plains, the pastor made a few comments and then announced that there would be singing. Mabel played a dozen carols, enjoying the sound of her neighbors' voices as they encouraged each other with joyful songs. At the end of each piece, she scanned the church for Mr. and Mrs. Spencer. Each time, Harper caught her eye and shook his head.

During one short break as Mabel found the

sheet music for the next tune, she heard Patty crying quietly. Patty hid her face against the wall and sobbed a few words, "Please God, let them come. I think I understand what hope is. I can feel it when I play music. I want them to feel hope too." Mabel reached over and squeezed Patty's hand, silently adding a prayer of her own.

As the night got later, the minister signaled for just one more song. "Now, Patty. It's our turn," Mabel said. "Will you play with me?" She took Patty's hand and led her to the bench, thankful that she didn't ask if her parents were there. In her last glance, Mabel hadn't seen them.

Mabel placed Patty's hands on the keys. Just as she began to count the rhythm, she heard the door open, and the floorboards creaked as someone entered. Slowly, the little girl began to play the simple melody. *O come, O come, Emmanuel, and ransom captive Israel...* Mabel joined her, playing a sweeping accompaniment. *O come, Thou Dayspring, come and cheer...* The congregation sang, their voices rising each time they repeated the chorus. *Rejoice! Rejoice! Emmanuel shall come to thee O Israel.*

In that small town, people had known the burden of despair. Some did not know where next week's food would come from. The music reminded them they were not the only ones who had struggled, and that Christ was still a Savior – born to bring hope. When their duet ended, there was a beautiful silence. Mabel hugged Patty and looked up at the two people approaching the piano bench.

"Did my parents come? To hear hope."

"We came," Mr. Spencer said, bending down and picking up his daughter.

"I'm here too," Mrs. Spencer announced, kissing Patty's cheek. "Harper told us to come. That it would be special. And it is. We're late because we had a long talk on the church steps."

"I'll be home a lot more. And we might even move to California to find work," Mr. Spencer said with a sober smile.

"Do you know what hope is?" Patty asked her parents. "It's joy, deep inside. When you know that better days are coming."

STARS IN THE WINDOW

1944

WORLD WAR II

STARS IN THE WINDOW

Sally wanted to snap off the radio with its cheery holiday songs. Something was wrong. She was certain. The rest of the family did not seem to feel the same way, though. Mom rolled the cookie dough with her usual calm precision. Pops whistled as he headed out to the barn. Fourteen-year-old Helen still neglected her chores to peacock in front of the mirror while ten-year-old Jerry enthusiastically read the battle accounts in the newspaper.

There hadn't been a letter for weeks. There was fighting in Europe. Sally had thought winter's snow would end the battles for a few weeks, but according to the news reports, the Germans had launched a counterattack which had pushed the Allied forces back.

The eighteen-year-old girl paused while putting away the dishes to run her hand over the map and push-pins Pops and Jerry used to mark the positions of the armies and to remind them to pray for victory. Her fingers lingered over the thin defensive positions in France. Somewhere along those stretching lines, Don and Jim were crouching low, battling for others' freedom. She hoped...

A sharp knock on the kitchen door startled her. "Can you get that, Sally?" Mom asked, as she slid a tray of gingerbread cookies into the oven.

Sally opened the door with a smile. "Why, Aunt Linda! How good to see you. Won't you come in?"

"Hello, dear," Aunt Linda replied, stepping in briskly and giving Sally a hug. "Hello, Dorothy," she greeted, then exclaimed before Mom had a chance to answer, "What are you doing? You know sugar's rationed. How can you be baking cookies?"

"I've saved our rations for several months, just to bake for the holidays. I didn't get it by stealing or cheating, Linda. Relax. Now that it's just two days 'til Christmas, I decided I'd better start baking."

"Well, good," Aunt Linda said, plopping down in a chair. "I came over just as soon as I could. You see, I was at the post office and..."

"There was a letter from the boys!" Sally exclaimed, clapping her hands expectantly.

"Don't interrupt, dear. Now, as I was saying," Aunt Linda continued, "I was at the post office, and I received a letter from dear Fred." She said it with such satisfied complacency that Sally momentarily wanted to choke her aunt. Coming over to tell them about Cousin Fred who had got some safe military job here in the states when she knew that Don and Jim were overseas! "He's doing wonderful. And even has a girlfriend."

"Hmm... Is that right?" Mom answered. Sally could tell she was pretending to be interested. Fred and a girlfriend was hardly news; he'd had girlfriends since he was fourteen.

"Aunt Linda, were there any letters for us?"

"No, dear. Oh...that's right. Don't tell me. You haven't heard from Don and Jim yet? My, my. I sure hope they're okay. How are you managing, Dorothy? I'd just be worried sick if I didn't hear from Freddy twice a week."

Mom just smiled half-heartedly. "One day at a time with lots of prayer."

An hour later, Aunt Linda left, and Sally retreated upstairs. Lying face down on her bed, she stifled her sobs in a pillow. For the last eight days, she hadn't slept well. She had a constant feeling that her brothers needed prayer. That all wasn't well. Sally worried especially about her twin, Jim. Something was wrong. There hadn't been letters. And now the reports of winter fighting. With tears on her face, Sally eventually fell asleep while the late afternoon sunlight spread comforting warmth in the room.

"Sally, Mom says it's time to get up." Someone shook her shoulder, and, when Sally opened her eyes, Helen smiled at her. "We're going to the Parker's for the party. Remember? How do you like my new hairstyle. Pops says I'm getting to be quite a young lady."

"It looks nice. I'll put on my best dress and be down in a moment," Sally said, rubbing her eyes and hoping it didn't look like she'd been crying.

"Do you think Jim and Don will even recognize me when they get home?" Helen questioned, leaning back into the room from the doorway.

"Yes, of course, silly." Satisfied, Helen closed the door. "But will we recognize them?" Sally wondered, sitting down in front of the small mirror, smoothing her hair, and fastening a Christmas pin to her checkered dress.

Downstairs, Sally couldn't help smiling as she saw their Christmas tree in the front room. Pops had gone down to the creek, dug up a small tree, wrapped the roots in a sack and set it up in the corner. They'd decided not to buy a traditional tree and had invested that money toward war bonds instead. Last evening, they had decorated the bare branches with strung popcorn, ornaments, and sprinkled tinsel.

"Ready to go?" Pops called. "Make sure you bundle up well. And are ya'll wearing walking shoes? It's a full-moon tonight and just a hop, skip, and a jump over to the Parker's, so we'll walk and save the gasoline and tires."

Sally slipped on her coat and wound the scarf around her head. As she headed for the door, she paused near the front window where two blue stars had been hung, representing her absent brothers. Sally's gloved fingers brushed over the thick paper and quickly traced the stars. "I wish you were here," she whispered, before heading into the crisp cold world.

"Don't you miss all the cute guys?" one of the neighbor girls giggled at the party.

"Oh, yes," Helen replied, but Sally nudged her and gave a warning look. Mom didn't like them to gossip or flirt.

"Have you heard from your brothers?" another young lady asked.

"No," Helen answered, turning pale. Then she smiled brightly, "But I'm sure they're fine. Probably at a wonderful party, dancing and laughing. I'm going to be so grown up when they get home, they'll have to take me to the dances down at Mr. Fairfield's."

Sally frowned and walked away. How could her little sister be so callous and uncaring? Didn't she realize what these weeks of silence could mean? Sally leaned against a window, looking into the night. "God keep them safe," she murmured. "And help us to know they're alright."

"Everything okay, Sis?" Jerry asked, his blue eyes sparkling with excitement. "Wait 'til you see the war board Jack and Hap made. It's even better than our push-pins on the map. They can plan real strategy. It's just like a game."

"War's not a game," Sally snapped. Then she saw the façade slip. Jerry's happiness crumpled, and tears started in his eyes. "I'm sorry. I shouldn't have been so harsh."

"I know war's not a game. It's just when I think about it too much, I get so worried about Skip and Doodle." He used the brotherly nicknames for their soldiers. "If I didn't follow the campaigns on the maps and believe we're going to win, I'd just crawl under a haystack and cry 'til I starved."

Sally pulled her little brother into a close embrace, fighting back her own tears. "Go on then. Keep believing. I believe we'll win too."

"And Skip and Doodle will come home."

"Yes. They'll come home," Sally answered, trying to trust despite the ever-growing doubts.

Late that evening as they neared their own home, Sally looked for the stars in the window with some superstitious fear that if they had slipped down something was really wrong. But both stars in the window hung as boldly as ever.

Upstairs, with the black-out shades in place,

Helen turned on a light and started untwisting her hair. "It's over."

"What's over?" Sally asked, sitting on the bed and rubbing her aching feet.

"I didn't cry. Not even when they asked about them," Helen went on. "I don't believe it. But I hope they are dancing and laughing with some friendly French girls."

"They'll come back, Helen. And they'll be proud to take us to the dances. Just think, we'll get to go with the handsomest guys who ever wore a U.S. uniform. They'll come back," she said again.

"You really think that?" Helen insisted harshly. "Don't look away, Sally. And don't lie to me. Where do you think they are?"

"I don't know," Sally whispered. "There are times I think they are... Then there are times I'm sure they're alive. And there are times I dream they come home for Christmas. I don't know. I don't know." She hid her face in her hands. "I wish I could be calm like Mom and Pops. The waiting is killing me."

For Sally, it was another restless night. Her thoughts teetered between the best and the worst. Her prayers alternated between pleading and resignation.

In the morning, she found Mom writing letters to the boys. "They'll want to hear from us, even though they haven't had time to write. I sure hope they received the Christmas package I sent."

"That's right, Dorothy," Pops said, setting down his coffee cup. "You know, I had a real good dream last night. It was summer, and the boys were home. And we were all fishin' down at the creek."

"Good," Mom said brightly. "We won't give up.

Just wait, pray, and trust God."

"And keep our own flag flying, and continue supporting the war effort," Pops added. "Speaking of which, I told Arnold I'd help him take apart his old, broken-down tractor for scrap metal. I'll be back early for supper since it's Christmas Eve."

They keep busy, Sally thought. We all do, in our own ways.

In the afternoon, Mom, Sally, and Helen were in the kitchen, finishing the preparations for the next day's fancy meal. It wouldn't be Christmas dinner like other years, but they'd managed to plan special treats with creativity and careful rationing. A brisk knock echoed on the door. "If it's Aunt Linda..." Sally threatened under her breath as she went to the door.

"Oh, my dears. You'll never guess. I just got the sweetest Christmas card from Fred's girlfriend. Let me read it to you!" Aunt Linda insisted, unwinding her scarf and pulling off her mitts.

"Happy Christmas Eve," Mom and Helen greeted.

Sally couldn't stand it. She grasped Aunt Linda's hands, saying sweetly with desperate hope, "Please, Aunt, you've been to the post office. Was there anything for us?"

"Oh...come to think of it. Mrs. Sims did mention there was a letter or two."

"And did you bring it?"

"Ouch! Dear, you mustn't squeeze my hands so hard. No, I didn't think to bring them. I don't think the post office would let me do that. Would they? Do you think?"

Sally looked at Mom. "Yes! Go," Mom ordered.

She impulsively kissed Aunt Linda's cheek,

pulled on a warm sweater, and dashed out the door. Sally climbed on their bicycle, thankful there wasn't any snow. It would make the mile trip to town easier. Pedaling as fast as she could in her skirt and heeled shoes, Sally steered the bicycle down the dirt lane, avoiding the worst ruts and holes. "Please, God, please," she said over and over. "Don't let it be from the army department. Don't let it have a black edge."

In town, she sped by the stores with their holiday displays, passed the church with wreaths and ribbon festooning the doors, and screeched to a halt at the post office, accidentally startling some ladies window shopping nearby. Sally's legs felt weak as she pushed open the door. Her breathing was panicky as she leaned against the counter and said, "Letters. I heard there were letters for my family."

"Oh, yes, dear. Just one though," Mrs. Sims replied, putting on her glasses. "From France, I think," she added as she handed Sally the precious envelope.

"Thank you," Sally breathed. "And Merry Christmas."

Outside, she sank down on the step and carefully opened the envelope. Her hands trembled as she drew out the single sheet of paper. It was dated from the beginning of the month. They were well.

"Thank you, God. Thank you," Sally murmured. She raced for home, anxious to share the letter with the family.

As Sally turned into the lane leading to the house, she caught her breath. The date. It was before the German counterattack. She shivered.

The letter had been comforting, but ultimately hadn't answered any questions. She climbed off the bicycle and leaned it against the porch.

Slowly, Sally climbed each step. The American flag hung still in the winter air. She reached up and pulled it open, to see every star and stripe. A moment later, she let go and climbed the last two steps to the porch. "It will always be like this," Sally whispered. "I'll always wonder, worry, hope, and believe. It will always be like this," she repeated. "Every Christmas. Every day. As long as there are stars in the window."

AN UNBROKEN CIRCLE

1970

VIETNAM CONFLICT

Sarah Kay Bierle

AN UNBROKEN CIRCLE

December 2013

"Frank G. Culver." Chris read the name aloud as he placed the evergreen wreath against the white marble tombstone. Reaching out to straighten the crimson bow, his fingers brushed against the inscription. Born 1948, Died 1970. A Vietnam soldier? he wondered. What was his story? Twenty-two, Chris thought. Close to my own age.

An older lady wearing a long black coat approached. Seeing her, Chris stepped aside, watching as she knelt and slipped three sprigs of delicate baby's breath into the wreath. "Do you know why I'm doing this?" she asked, her voice quavering. Chris shook his head. "For the three children he saved."

December 1970

They all knew it. The Vietcong were advancing in the area. The mutters among messmates revealed doubts about the situation in South Vietnam. They were being sent out on patrol again, and tempers were short.

In the corner of the tent, Frank leaned against an empty crate, ignoring the cursing jibes and coarse talk of his comrades. He was the lucky one today – many days, actually: he had letters at mail call. His sister – Diane – and his mom were the best correspondents, keeping him informed of the local news and sending words of encouragement. He'd stopped reading the papers long ago – didn't want to know about the rebellion, politics, and weak support in his country. He'd stopped thinking about the causes of the war too. All that mattered was obeying God and obeying orders. He still didn't know if he thought the draft was fair, but he knew his life depended on his comrades, and they depended on him.

In the last months, his faith had been his stronghold. Huddled in the unforgiving terrain or marching through the muddy jungle, the only way to calm his taut nerves was reciting Scripture verses. At night as he mouthed the encouraging words, he could rest and imagine he was home for a brief moment, strolling into the little Baptist church, ready for a Sunday service or Wednesday Bible study.

He folded the letter and slipped it in his pack. Diane cheerily wished him a Merry Christmas. He'd almost forgotten about the holiday. Days ran together endlessly here. He closed his eyes, trying to imagine her happy smile and the way she sang carols in her high, out-of-key voice. Home was thousands of miles away, and, with the promised patrol, it seemed the only Christmas he'd get this year was what he chose to remember. There wouldn't even be the opportunity to celebrate in camp.

Hours later, they were tramping through the countryside. Sergeant Jones marched in front of him, his rifle at the ready and his helmeted head turning slowly as he scanned the area. Frank gripped his weapon and shrugged slightly, trying to ease the weight of his pack; intently, he listened and watched, fully expecting enemy gunfire at any moment. Behind him, his buddy Rich Patterson – nicknamed "Scruffy" – trudged, panting and whispering "blast it!" every time he stepped in a muddy patch. The other soldiers spread out behind, all alert.

Days went by with no sign of the Vietcong. "Maybe we'll get lucky this time," Scruffy muttered one night as he and Frank hunkered at the base of a tree. "Drats, it's Christmas Eve too!" He flopped over and hid his face. Frank didn't reply. He'd been bivouac buddies with Rich long enough to note the catch in his comrade's voice.

Why did You come to earth, God? he wondered. Frank mentally listed salvation, mercy, forgiveness, fulfill prophecy – testing himself to remember a Scripture verse to support each point. Love, he thought – that was the ultimate reason. *For God so loved the world...Greater love has no man than this, than to lay down one's life for his friends...* The thought was comforting and yet a paradox. This Christmas would be war and killing on too many battlefronts. He shook his head and closed his eyes.

Dawn came. It wasn't beautiful and pristine. No voices sang a carol, no gifts were exchanged. A few soldiers mumbled a holiday greeting, but most ignored the day. Frank knew better than to wish his comrades a Merry Christmas. He merely touched the cross hanging with his dog tags. "Let me show them. Not tell them, Lord." He checked his weapon and fingered the extra ammunition in his belt. "Love, Forgiveness, Faithfulness. Unbroken circle of grace." It was just another day of patrol.

At dusk, the gunfire erupted and vanished. They crept after their unseen foes. The jungle broke, and bullets blazed from a barricaded village in the clearing. Fight to survive instincts and the brutal training and experience took over. Frank crouched behind a tree and gritted his teeth, shooting back at the hidden enemy. Screams and shouts of pain punctuated the combat noise. Panting, Frank rammed another ammunition clip into his gun. "Forgive me, God," he groaned. "This is not the way to show them."

"Their fire power's less. Let's go. Pass the word," the sergeant shouted. Moments later, the Americans darted from the cover of the trees, moving across the open ground. Bullets whizzed around them, and Frank didn't look. Didn't want to see who fell in the deep twilight of Christmas night.

Scruffy shadowed Frank as he reached one of the sandbag piles, the sergeant just behind him. Frank hoisted himself over the barricade, waiting for the fatal shot from an enemy. It didn't come. Five people stood in the darkness with their hands in the air. Warily, Frank watched them, not trusting anyone in these situations. More Americans crawled over the sandbags. No shots. Nothing.

Then the whirl of bullets came with the crack of

rifle fire. Reflexively, Frank dropped to the ground. "After them. Clear the houses," the sergeant bellowed. Attack was the only way to survive this trap. If they stayed there, they were sitting ducks. Frank and the sergeant crawled to the closest of the four huts, took cover, and searched the single room. Nothing. His pounding heart still seemed to skip beats, expecting a shot from the dark corners. "It's empty," he said.

Shouting and furious screaming erupted outside, followed by a staccato sentence of death. Frank turned in the doorway, seeing a line of bodies on the ground. "No civilian deaths!" the sergeant barked, running toward the scene.

"These ain't civilians," Scruffy argued back, his voice breaking. "She shot Wilkes." He kicked the woman's corpse. "Just kill them all."

Frank's anger flashed. A movement caught his eye. Tiny figures ran from the next hut toward the dead. Scruffy turned his gun toward the scurrying shadows. The world seemed to lock into slow motion. A burst of deadly flashes exploded around them. Frank dropped his weapon and took a running leap forward, diving toward the ground, and knocking the children down to safety. His arms and body shielded them. And then the pain came.

"What..." The firing stopped, and pounding boots approached. "Oh my..." Scruffy's voice cut off abruptly. "Culver!"

"They were only children," Frank panted, struggling for breath as Scruffy knelt beside him. "You would've shot kids, man." The sergeant came while the other soldiers finished raking the village and torched the buildings. Under his arms and body, Frank felt the writhing kids. "Roll me over. I can't move," he pleaded.

"You're shot, Culver," Scruffy finally said, digging into his pockets for a field dressing.

The flames rose higher, consuming the huts and casting illuminating light on the destructive scene. The children sat up, crying. "It's alright," Frank whispered, staring at their small faces. Above him, Scruffy and the sergeant exchanged horrified glances.

"Why'd you do it?" the sergeant asked through gritted teeth as he tore open Frank's jacket, exposing the chest wound.

Frank gasped. "They were just children." He tried to turn away from the pressure Scruffy applied to the bleeding injury. "Look at them, Sarge. The oldest can't be more than seven." He bit his lip and tried to blink back the tears from the pain. "It's Christmas."

He looked back at the children. The oldest girl had inched closer and now leaned over his head, watching with dark, curious eyes. "You're beautiful," Frank murmured. "Take care of them now, Scruffy." The pain was fading. His vision tunneled, focusing on the little girl. He couldn't put his thoughts into words, but he struggled for each breath and made it count. "It's Christmas. Forgive. God...so love. Lay down life. For friends. It's Christ..." The words whirled into the coming darkness. It was time to sleep. He felt a tiny hand on his face.

December 2014

Rebecca Smith climbed out of her car, clutching the piece of paper with the information she'd been given. Months earlier, she'd received a response to the message she had posted years before on a Vietnam history forum. She had always longed to know the name of the soldier who had thrown her to the ground and away from the bullets. If she closed her eyes, Rebecca could vividly remember his still, quiet face.

Frank G. Culver. That was his name. His sister had called one day, and, after comparing Rebecca's faint remembrances with the known details, they were certain Frank had saved her.

Today, she had driven several hours to reach the cemetery. Her adopted parents were watching her children for her since her husband had to work; from the very first day they met her when she walked off a plane in America, they'd given her love and support. They had been glad to hear she was discovering more about her earliest years in her home country.

Taking a deep breath, she walked toward the gravestone.

Ben Trung wiped his sweaty hands on his coat. As a reporter, he'd outgrown fear long ago and was comfortable talking to people. But today he'd see his brother for the first time in decades. They had been messaging, ever since Diane had given them each other's contact information.

Frank G. Culver. That was the soldier who had saved his life one December night. He could remember the fires and a man shielding him, but not much more. He had only been three at the time. He barely remembered the flight to America, but he could clearly recall the moment he met his adoptive parents. For the first time, he had felt safe.

Straightening his tie, he walked toward the gravestone.

Nicholas Turner rubbed his eyes. Jet lag was still troubling him. He'd flown in that morning. He was going to see his real brother. He had siblings in his adopted American family, but this was different: his real brother. It had been a shock when he got an email a few weeks ago from a woman named Diane Stockton. She had told him the story and the researched reasons they thought he was the third child. She had asked him to come. She had "introduced" him to his brother.

Frank G. Culver. He'd been told this American soldier saved his life. He didn't remember anything from that night. Two years old. His clearest memory was an American Christmas, a year or two after he was adopted from the orphanage.

Grasping a small Bible, he walked toward the gravestone.

"I don't know if I can do this," Diane whispered, wiping her eyes with her handkerchief. "I only told you that story last year because I wanted someone else to know. My husband had always come with me, but that was my first year without him."

"It's going to be alright," Chris promised, parking the car. "This is going to be a special moment."

"All because you know how to research and find clues and people." She smiled as she climbed out of the car. "You've become like family too, putting those research skills to use and talking with me."

Together, they walked toward the gravestone. Diane carried a wreath and baby's breath.

After a few moments of greetings, tears, and conversation, the group continued their walk through the rows of gravestones. "Someone's there," Diane said, seeing an older gentleman standing reflectively near Frank's grave.

He looked up as they approached. "I had to come today. And ask you to forgive me. I'm Rich Patterson. They called me Scruffy in 1970. I saw Ben's blog post about his thoughts on coming here today. I had to come."

"Did you know Frank?" Diane asked.

"Did I know Frank..." the man repeated. "Yes. I marched behind him every day. Kept guard while he slept, and he did the same for me. But on Christmas Day 1970, it was..." He broke down and tried to turn away. Rebecca reached out and put her arms around him. Calming, he finished, "I was the soldier who fired the gun at the children. It was the bullets from my gun that hit Frank. Can you ever forgive me?" Diane, Ben, and Nicholas joined Rebecca in a group hug.

Rich cleared his throat. "On New Year's Day 1971, I gave my life to Christ. I'd never been religious. But Frank's last words impressed me so strongly that the first thing I did after that patrol was find a chaplain to help me understand what Frank meant."

"What did he say?" Nicholas asked.

Rich knelt down beside the white marble gravestone. "I remember it like it was yesterday. He said, 'It's Christmas. Forgive. God so love. Lay down life. For friends. It's Christ...'"

Diane handed him the evergreen wreath, and he gently placed it. Rebecca, Ben, and Nicholas bent and arranged the white flowers. Then they stood, holding hands around the gravestone of their hero. Chris drew back. This was their time.

"It's an unbroken circle, by God's grace," Nicholas said. "Frank saved us that night because God had a plan."

"Amen," Rich murmured.

"I think Frank would've liked music," Rebecca whispered. "Do you think we could sing?" They nodded.

Then let us all with one accord
Sing praises to our heavenly Lord
That hath made Heaven and earth of nought
And with his blood mankind has bought.
Noel, Noel, Noel, Noel
Born is the King of Israel!

Elsewhere, the world bustled on with its holiday hilarity, trying to find superficial gifts for the season. If those people had only stopped to look, they would've seen a testimony of love and they could've learned what it really meant to give. Against a white marble headstone lay an unbroken circlet of evergreens accented with baby's breath and tied with a crimson bow: this soldier had shown what Christmas really meant.

"A MESSAGE WE WOULD LIKE TO SEND TO YOU"

MODERN ERA

"A MESSAGE WE WOULD LIKE
TO SEND TO YOU"

Almost got it, I thought, chasing the little icon with my finger on the phone screen. Deeply absorbed in the game, I could almost ignore the holiday. Christmas had lost its sparkle and wonder to my thirteen year old mind; I didn't know if it was because I missed Grandma, or if I was too old to enjoy the evening.

The Christmas tree glittered with lights and ornaments. Holiday music filtered through the house. Mom was in the kitchen, making a happy clatter as she finished the preparations for tomorrow's feast. But I just felt like the whole celebration was superficial and useless. As fake as pretending the tinsel was real gold. Sure, the minister would talk about Jesus and peace, but then what? The excitement was for the little kids. Grandma wasn't even here to read the Christmas story like she always had. Dad had said he would, but it just wasn't going to be the same. I wasn't sure what I wanted to celebrate, and, by hiding behind my phone, I didn't have to think about any of it.

"Honey," Mom called to Dad, "I'm so sorry, but I forgot to get three apples, and I really need them for the coffee cake. Could you..."

"Yes, of course. I'll run to the store," Dad replied. "We'll read the story later," he promised nine-year-old Kathy and seven-year-old Luke. I glanced up from the game, hoping my younger siblings weren't going to start being noisy.

"Can Grandpa read to us?" Luke clamored, running toward the comfortable chair where Grandpa sat, balancing a mug of wassail and writing in his journal.

"In a little while," he replied gruffly. "I'm almost done."

As Dad pulled on his coat and headed out to the car, Kathy came to me. "Go 'way," I said. "I'm busy."

"Jeff, please put your phone away," Mom said, looking into the living room. "It's Christmas Eve, and it's family time. I'll be finished soon, and we'll play a game or something."

Huffing, I put my electronic device on the shelf where phones went when we weren't using them. My siblings were starting to argue about which cookie tasted better: gingerbread or almond. What did it matter? I thought, rolling my eyes. "Oh, stop it, you two," I ordered. "If you don't behave better, Mom and Dad won't let you have your presents tomorrow."

"Presents!" Luke squealed.

"Yes, presents. Tomorrow's Christmas," Kathy echoed.

That started it. The kids began dancing around singing "Jingle Bells", asking when we were going to church, and wondering what toys they would receive in the morning. Suddenly, Luke announced he was going to be an astronaut and dashed upstairs to get his costume. His reasoning? If he was an astronaut, he could fly to where Christmas was already happening. Kathy chased after him, explaining how that wouldn't work.

"Christmas," I groaned aloud.

"Yes, Christmas," Grandpa responded meditatively, closing his journal and setting it aside. "I was writing about your grandmother and how she loved the holiday. It makes me feel better, remembering all those wonderful years we had together. I told you I left poinsettias at the cemetery before I made the trip here, didn't I?"

"Yes, Grandpa," I replied awkwardly. I didn't really want to talk about Grandma; Christmas had been her favorite, and I missed her happiness and how she found a way to make the holiday meaningful for everyone. From upstairs, the whirling patter of feet announced the coming reappearance of Luke and Kathy. I rolled my eyes again, but Grandpa smiled indulgently.

"Astronaut! Astronaut! I'm an astronaut," Luke hollered, running around the room and jumping on and off the footstool.

Kathy followed with a foam dart gun. "I'm going to get the astronaut who's spoiling Christmas," she threatened.

"Luke, Kathy, settle down," Mom reprimanded. "And stop jumping on the ottoman. I'm almost finished, I promise," a hint of frustration in her tone. "Jeff, could you find some Christmas coloring pages or something to do with Luke and Kathy?"

"How about a story?" Grandpa said, his quiet voice contrasting with the noisy scene. Luke made a face and kept running around the room. "A story about my favorite Christmas? A story about astronauts?" he hinted.

Luke paused. "Astronauts?"

"I want a Christmas story, please," Kathy pleaded.

"My story is about Christmas and astronauts," Grandpa answered, setting aside his empty cup. "Come on, sit down. You too, Jeff. Come join us."

Sitting on the floor, we watched as Grandpa paged through his journal. "This is my Christmas diary," he explained. "I just have to check the year, and then the rest of the story I can tell from memory. I'll never forget it."

"Christmas diary?" Kathy asked.

"Yep. I write a little every Christmas Eve so I can remember what I was doing and thinking. Ready for the story?"

Kathy and Luke were enthusiastic. I just nodded politely.

"It was Christmas 1968. I think you children know that I worked in NASA's space program? That December the space mission Apollo 8 was sent to orbit the moon. Three astronauts were onboard the space capsule. Frank Borman, Jack Lovell, and William Anders."

"Were they in space for Christmas?" Kathy asked.

"Shh...I'm getting there," Grandpa said, smiling. "Well, that Christmas Eve Grandma and I were home in our little house. We'd just gotten married that year, and it was our first Christmas. Unfortunately, my job had us living far away from our relatives, and we didn't have the money to travel. But it was alright. We had decorated a little and were going to have Christmas Day brunch after church with some of our friends. We had a little tiny television set, and, at the right hour, I turned it on because the astronauts on Apollo 8 were supposed to give a holiday message."

Grandpa sighed and went on. "Grandma and I were sitting there in our folding chairs. (We couldn't afford a couch yet.) I was holding her hand, and we had been talking about the meaning of Christmas: Jesus coming to earth. When the program started, we could hear the faint, crackly voices of the astronauts in space. They showed pictures of the earth and moon and described the scene. Lovell described it as, 'The vast loneliness is awe-inspiring, and it makes you realize just what you have back there on Earth.' "

"Wow," Luke whispered.

"What did you think, Grandpa?" I asked.

"Oh, the story's not finished yet. We heard Ander's voice say: 'For all the people on Earth the crew of Apollo 8 has a message we would like to send you.' Then he began to read from the Bible. You might think he would've read the nativity account from the Gospel of Matthew or Luke, but they read something else instead. They went to the first book of the Bible." Grandpa paused. "I could recite it for you, but... Jeff, do you think you could find the Apollo 8 recording on your phone and play it for us?"

"Sure. Hey Mom," I called, "Grandpa wants me to find something on my phone for him. Can I use it?"

"Yes, then put it away again," she responded,

turning off the water at the kitchen sink.

A quick search and I'd found the video. Pushing play and turning up the volume, I listened to the faint crackling sound and wondered how many hundreds of miles these men were from home when they made the message.

Ander's voice said the introduction Grandpa had quoted, then began reading.

"In the beginning God created the heaven and the earth. And the earth was without form, and void; and darkness was upon the face of the deep. And the Spirit of God moved upon the face of the waters. And God said, Let there be light: and there was light. And God saw the light, that it was good: and God divided the light from the darkness."

"Lovell reads next," Grandpa whispered. Dad came in, carrying a grocery bag and stopped to listen.

"And God called the light Day, and the darkness he called Night. And the evening and the morning were the first day. And God said, Let there be a firmament in the midst of the waters, and let it divide the waters from the waters. And God made the firmament, and divided the waters which were under the firmament from the waters which were above the firmament: and it was so. And God called the firmament Heaven. And the evening and the morning were the second day."

Mom stepped into the room, listening. Grandpa cleared his throat. "Now, Borman."

"And God said, Let the waters under the heavens be gathered together unto one place, and let the dry land appear: and it was so. And God called the dry land Earth; and the gathering together of the waters called He Seas: and God

saw that it was good."

There was a short pause, and Borman concluded, "And from the crew of Apollo 8, we close with good night, good luck, a Merry Christmas, and God bless all of you – all of you on the good Earth."

I blinked and swallowed the tight feeling in my throat.

"Can we go out and see the stars?" Luke begged.

"Sure," Dad replied.

It was perfect, I thought, as we stood in a line, holding hands and looking up at the heavens. For a moment, all the decorations, the food, the lights, the music had faded from our focus. The superficial was overruled by profound truth and reflection. We were away from the earthly holiday glitter and seeing the sparkling beauty of God's creation. And we were together as a family, focusing our gaze and heart-felt praise.

Suddenly, Christmas had meaning again. I wanted to celebrate. I was awed by reality: God – the One who made the heavens and earth – had come to earth on that first Christmas.

"I didn't finish telling the story," Grandpa murmured. "And yet, I did. I think you all understand how I felt."

I squeezed Grandpa's hand. "In the beginning...God," I whispered.

Sarah Kay Bierle

HISTORICAL NOTES

Great Joy – Though the capital city was not specified and the incident is entirely fictional, the Christmas decorations mentioned in the story are based on the beautiful and natural wreaths, swags, and other arrangements displayed at Colonial Williamsburg during the holiday season.

Patriot Dreams – The Continental Army did not arrive at Valley Forge until December 19, 1777. Most of the ladies did not travel to Valley Forge until the early months of 1778; thus, this story is best read as a "winter tale." Martha Washington and Mrs. Greene are real historical figures with brief "cameo appearances." This story was very loosely based on a dramatic play I wrote several years ago.

East To West - "Trail of Tears" is a dark moment in America's past. Thousands of Native Americans were forcibly moved from their traditional lands and established communities to the western plains. Many died along the way, especially during the harsh winter months.

A Light In The Window – Following the Mexican-American War (1846-1848), the Californio residents of the new U.S. territory faced many conflicts. The setting for this story was inspired by memories of a childhood visit to Rancho Guajome Adobe during the Christmas season.

The Christmas Sermon –This tale was inspired by accounts that I found in my Gettysburg research about "ministers" wandering into field hospitals and wanting to preach, but having no interest in bringing water and food or re-bandaging wounds. (The wounded were not very complimentary of these "preach, but don't practice" chaplains.) The hospital and winter setting in the story reflects details from Louisa May Alcott's account "Hospital Sketches" and other primary sources.

Curses Or Blessings? – During the mid-19th Century, many Irish families left their homeland and immigrated to America. The great famines and social conflict forced them to seek a better life in a new land. Many young women found jobs as maids in wealthy houses.

Song Of Hope – My maternal grandfather was born in Texas during the Dust Bowl era. The details in this story were gleaned from some of his stories, but the characters and plot are original.

Stars In The Window – During World War II, families would hang stars in their front window to represent how many family members were serving in the armed forces. My great-grandfather (paternal) and his four brothers served; there were five stars in that home window. Incredibly, all five boys came home. Writing this story was a special and unforgettable experience; a lot of personal feeling found its way into the text. I have family and friends in the armed forces, and there is no way to describe the conflict of anxiety, trust, and hope when you just want to know they're okay. Never forget – there are still stars in the window...

An Unbroken Circle – Every year, I go to a national cemetery and help place evergreen wreaths with crimson bows on the grave markers. I wonder about the life and service of the person as I say their name aloud. In 1975, there were "operations" to bring orphaned Vietnamese children to America for safety and adoption. The Vietnam Conflict and veterans hold a special place in my heart; a study in college introduced me to the fierce battles, ethical and moral dilemmas, and personal struggles of the battlefields. Perhaps someday, I will find the courage to write more about this era. We must never forget the sacrifices and long-term challenges created by the conflict.

"A Message We Would Like To Send To You" – The quotes by the astronauts and the italicized Scripture verses are taken directly from a transcription of the original message. (Transcription found on NASA website).

ACKNOWLEDGEMENTS

With Gladness was a "surprise." Usually, I spend months (sometimes years) planning my stories and books. This book was first considered in July 2016 and goes to the printers in October 2016. I'd like to personally thank my team who never lets me quit on writing and editing projects.

Susan Bierle – my mom has believed in this book since the day I first mentioned it to her. She read the first drafts and gave constructive criticism on every story. And she sent me back to my desk to keep writing when I was exhausted and creatively bored. Thanks for everything, Mom!

Shawn Bierle – Dad, you took time from your busy schedule to read the manuscript and share your thoughts. I hope you have fun talking about the book at Christmas parties. ;)

Robert Rasband – my neighbor and amazing proof-reader told me about some problems in the stories, giving me a chance to improve before the text goes in print. Thank you for being honest and kind.

Ted & Cindy McCord – You have both encouraged me to write and always tell me that I will get to Colonial Williamsburg for Christmas ...someday. Thank you for sharing your lovely photography for the book cover!

ABOUT THE AUTHOR

Sarah Kay Bierle was homeschooled K-12, completed an accelerated distance learning program for college, and graduated from Thomas Edison State University with a BA in History. She manages her own company – planning historical events and publishing – and currently serves as an Assistant Blog Editor for Emerging Civil War.

Sarah believes in reading good literature and participating in hands-on learning to supplement traditional studying; she is grateful to her parents for allowing her to explore and learn. Her love of knowledge and teaching has prompted her to become involved in living history and blogging, where she shares her belief that "history is about real people, real actions, and real effects, and it should inspire us today."

When not researching or writing, Sarah enjoys spending time with her parents and siblings, volunteering, playing music, quilting, or visiting with close friends. She desires to share a message of hope in Christ through her daily life and her writing.

To order books,
find historical resources,
or contact the author,
please visit:

www.Gazette665.com